OPERATION BUTTERFLY

PROMISE ME A MIRACLE
BOOK ONE

NALEIGHNA KAI
MARTHA KENNERSON

MACRO PUBLISHING GROUP

Operation Butterfly - Book 1 of the Promise Me a Miracle Series

Copyright @ 2024 - Naleighna Kai and Martha Kennerson

Published by:

Macro Publishing Group

1507 E. 53rd Street, Suite 858

Chicago, Illinois

www.naleighnakai.com

Trade Paperback ISBN: 978-1-952871-94-8

Digital ISBN: 9781952871382

Cover Design by: Woodson Creative Studio

www.woodsoncreativestudio.com

Interior Design by: Lissa Woodson

www.naleighnakai.com

NALEIGHNA KAI
ACKNOWLEDGEMENTS

Dedicated to:

Renee Sesvalah Cobb Dishman,
   Jean Woodson,
   Eric Harold Spears,
   LaKecia Janise Woodson,
   Mildred E. Williams,
   Anthony Johnson,
   L. A. Banks,
   Octavia Butler,
   Tanishia Pearson Jones,
   Derek Fields
   Emmanuel McDavid,
   Evelyn Jeanette Woodson, and
   Priscilla Jackson.

Special thanks goes to: The Creator from whom all Blessings and opportunities flow, Sesvalah, my son, J. L. Woodson (for the awesome cover designs for the Knights of the Castle series, the Kings of the Castle series, Queens of the Castle series and The Days of Pleasure series), Janice M. Allen, Debra J. Mitchell, Royce Slade Morton, Bunny Ervin, Martha Kennerson, J. L. Campbell, Kelly Peterson, Janine A. Ingram, S. L. Jennings, Ehryck F. Gilmore, Mary B. Morrison, Auriella Skye, LaVerne Thompson, Kassanna Dwight, Vikkas Bhardwaj, Ellen Kiley Goeckler,

Stephanie M. Freeman, J. D. Mason, Unique Hiram, Shakir Rashaan, Ken Duncan, Jr., the Kings of the Castle Ambassadors, Members of Naleighna Kai's Literary Cafe, the members of NK Tribe Called Success, and to you, my dear readers . . . thank you all for your support.

Much love, peace, and joy,
 Naleighna Kai

MARTHA KENNERSON
ACKNOWLEDGEMENTS

It has been a great privilege to be a part of this project. I'd like to acknowledge my writing partner Naleighna Kai for allowing me to accompany her on this journey. I want to thank my amazing husband, Joe, who has supported me on my journey. And my three beautiful daughters.

CHAPTER 1

$\mathcal{F}$ourteen days before American's Mandatory Evacuation from Ajid

"You're about to get fired on your day off." Rustling sounds on the other end of the call was a hint that Dro Reyes was doing paperwork, something everyone knew he hated. He was speaking in King's Speak Protocol and still managing to multitask which was a miracle unto itself.

"Wait, you don't understand." Jaxon Malone pressed his forehead against the cool surface of the wall in a modestly furnished bedroom. He wondered how his mentor could do both while he was the one struggling to use a blend of five basic languages and a slight bit of Navajo code talk for the more sensitive parts so the distress call could not be intercepted.

Given the volatile state of Ajid and its rapidly deteriorating relations with America, he had to get Alia Fadel out of the country to some place safe. Dro's fiancée would go ballistic if her maid of honor wasn't in the United States by the time they were ready to say 'I do'."

"I most certainly do understand," Dro countered in that signature voice that spoke of the calm before a raging storm. "According to you, Ajid was a hop, skip, and a jump from where your assignment was at the time. You said, and I quote, 'you can count on me to bring Lola's best friend to the States for your wedding, and on time.'"

"I know what I said, but Dro, listen to me." Jax groaned, remembering how optimistic he was when accepting what was supposed to be a simple two-hour mission into the Middle East to escort the raven-haired beauty onto a private flight. This would reunite her with a mother she had not seen in over a year, and then on to Dro and Lola's holiday wedding. That simple thought seemed like ages ago with an eternity thrown in for good measure. No way could he—or anyone—have known that the world would change so drastically or that she would be prohibited from leaving the country.

The new regime also heavily penalized Alia's family for not handing her to authorities for participating in protests about Oded Farhat, the man who had unlawfully seized power. He was disregarding the treaties regarding women in this country that was forged by an earlier Malik Bashir's regime.

"She had a new position at Meridian lined up and that opportunity has come and gone," Dro said while shuffling papers. A light tap on the desk made it clear Dro was now intently focused on the phone call, probably wearing that "disappointed parent expression" Jax dreaded.

As a fixer and the founder of Vantage Point, Dro was used to handling bad news and even worse situations. But when it came to Lola, his future wife, he had been nothing short of a prowling lion. Right now, Jax had to take his head out of the lion's mouth one inch at a time.

"See, we have a bit of a problem," Jax admitted, adjusting his chair so he had a better view of the garden Alia's father had planted to feed the family now that food sources were drying up.

"We shouldn't have a bit of a problem," Dro shot back in a measured tone.

The gnawing ache in Jax's side made him look towards the bed he shared with Alia in a back bedroom away from the prying eyes of the rest of the family. The thought of her soft skin against his made other parts of his body ache. Their current circumstances fit in with everything else that was wrong with his life at the moment.

This morning when she awakened, she was trying to be brave, but the tremors flowing through her sweet body affected him. Time was winding down and the odds weren't just stacked against them, the damn things were multiplying with each passing moment. They had taken Alia's passport and ripped it into pieces. She had kept the fragments, but the next checkpoint wouldn't let her through with those.

"I've been trying to negotiate Alia's travel with the Ministry of Defense, and they've been giving us hell since everything's now in chaos." Jax moved to their bed, snagged one of Alia's pashminas, and pressed the silken fabric to his nose, inhaling the scent of jasmine and apricot. Combined with Alia's own sensual perfume his emotions went into overdrive with fear leading the pack.

"What's the issue?" Dro asked and his tone was all business—right where Jax needed it to be.

"Another source confirmed that there was some type of vendetta we knew nothing about before you sent me here. With the Farhats seizing power the way they did, leaving will be damn near impossible."

"They can do that to an American citizen? Restrict her travel that way?"

The disbelief in Dro's voice annoyed Jax. Taking a woman's passport and restricting her travel was one of a catalog of rules and systems that reared their ugly heads. The level of control Oded Farhat had was gaining traction so fast that no one—not even the United Nations—had time to adjust. And all of this was totally unchecked by the American military who were present in the country but had been directed to stand down since their date for total evacuation was already set. This was a startling reversal given the fact that the United States had encouraged women, especially Zaras—to become vital parts of the military and the police force. The Zaras were an ethnic group that had been targeted and persecuted by the Ajidis for centuries. Though they shared the same religion as the Ajidis, they occupied lands and resources that the Ajidis covet and caused them to be the target of ethnic cleansing. But now that the old regime—the Balitan had overtaken the country, both groups were in danger—women and Zaras.

Jax was all too aware of the fragile situation in this part of the world. Sure, the press fractured the truth a bit, but the essence of what they reported was the same. He had witnessed a man and his wife being dragged out of the airport before the officers dropped them on the ground like garbage. All because the husband had the audacity to defend his wife against Oded's military. She also happened to be a woman who led demonstrations against the sweeping changes. Not only was this happening way ahead of the officially agreed time for the United States to leave, but it came from Oded who had usurped power and sent Malik Bashir, the previous ruler, fleeing for his life and putting America's determination for a peaceful evacuation to a rigid test.

The moment American troops began their partial evacuation, Farhat had activated military from the neighboring countries and swept in from the outskirts overtaking village by village. Then went inward to the cities before finally capturing the tribunal headquarters and the surrounding palaces. Their actions of trying to shake off the influence of Western culture were sending women —and especially the Zaras—back to the stone ages were absolute. As though someone wanted to pull the curtain down on freedom and block out every sliver of light.

"I just found out from a source a few moments before our call that all of the challenges regarding Alia are coming from Oded personally. Alia's father, Nasir, is at a severe disadvantage because he did not openly favor Oded over Malik. Now his wealth is dwindling to pennies because some underhanded moves are in play. I've spent a lot of my own cash trying to grease the right palms, but I keep hitting roadblocks as well. The fines from Alia's arrest after the protest are unfairly exorbitant. They keep extending her court date and the amount we owe keeps piling on every day, and so are the lawyer fees. Even with that, others were not so fortunate and remain behind bars. Some of those women have died in custody or disappeared altogether."

Jax flopped down on the bed and placed the rich purple fabric aside. "They put an option on the table to make it stop, but what they ask is impossible. Not to mention, someone inside this family must be telegraphing our every move because they are always three steps ahead. Intel says they're holding a seat on the tribunal out as a reward for male family members who make sure their families fall in line or ones who are reporting the whereabouts of the women officers in hiding.

"I have an idea who, but it doesn't look like Alia will be leaving here until someone else can pull some strings from the outside. She definitely needs another American passport."

"You said they offered a compromise of some sort," Dro said. "What's the problem?"

Measuring his words carefully, Jax replied, "The main issue is she doesn't want to marry the new ruler. He's forcing this because he thinks that it would be an outward sign that what's been fed to the world about how they're treating the Zaras are lies."

Not that what Alia wanted mattered in their eyes. The social traditions in Ajid were nearly impractical to navigate. Sometimes an honor killing was a plausible solution to bring a rebellious woman to her knees. But if they laid a hand on Alia, it would be game over. Jax would level the palace and everyone in it.

"Could you call in the Kings—"

"Kings have already been told we can't get involved with local issues over there. Trying to wage anything against the Balitan regime could put American relations in jeopardy," Dro said after several moments. From the background noise, he had left The Castle and made it to his car. "Traditions and arranged marriages are a sacred thing no matter what politics are in play."

"That's not it," Jax said. "There was no marriage contract for Alia to marry him. They're forcing wealthy families who had not taken their side, into financial ruin for the sole reason of making them compliant. This marriage is part of that. Not to mention marrying a Zara human rights activist openly would put to bed the rumor that the recent massacre they committed was worse than the one twenty years ago."

Dro exhaled and Jax braced himself for even worse news. "Americans already have enough problems over there. We don't need to add a challenge with a dictator who isn't answering to anyone, certainly not the United States who helped rebuild their country. Not even the United Nations who immediately encouraged countries to call for sanctions the minute Oded's men overtook the capital."

"Let me state it differently," Jax said a little slower, as though Dro hadn't been following his explanation. "She *can't* marry him."

A lengthy pause from Dro ensued after those words as traffic sounds echoed on the other end. "All right, what am I missing here?"

"They're still putting these demands on the table because they don't know that she's already married."

"Come again?"

With his heart beating like a college drumline, Jax replied, "She's already married ... to me."

CHAPTER 2

$\mathcal{J}$ ax glanced at the simple gold band on the third finger of his left hand and frowned. Hasty nuptials meant to change Alia Fadel's identity and provide safe passage from Ajid to the U.S. had not gone according to plan. They were turned away at the first checkpoint when one of the guards said that Zaras were not allowed to leave the country without a passport and special visa. He ripped up the passport and tossed the pieces on the ground. They had to scramble to pick them up before he released a shot in the air for them to keep moving.

His mentor's silence behind that statement was frightening. "Dro?"

"So, a man who swore up and down he would *never, ever* get married did it anyway, right? You barely know the woman and her family, and somehow managed to marry her out from under a powerful man who's aiming to have her for himself? A high-ranking member of this new regime?"

"See, and his ears and brain work too," was the only thing Jax could come up with, hoping to lighten the mood.

Dro's dry, bitter laugh made Jax bristle. Not exactly the lightness he was going for in the conversation. Jax angled to an adjacent window and looked out to find the village was one bustling with the activity of people trying to leave for "sudden visits" to families in neighboring countries. Chatter from the streets and the scent of spices filled the air. But it was also easy to recognize the men tucked in the shadows watching Nasir's house and reporting back to Oded.

"That is no small problem," Dro replied with a bit of censure in his tone. "Do you realize they will kill her and you, too?"

Yes, he was more than aware of the danger they now faced. Possibility and reality had exchanged places during one of his treks to the market securing the items for the next day's meals and giving him the opportunity to get a feel for how others were being impacted. Those who had planned to flee the country under American military protection weren't aware of everything Oded had done under the cover of darkness. Everyone believed that they had several months, but the invasion had escalated so fast that their suitcases weren't even packed. Retribution was swift. Women were being hit the hardest. Zaras were hit even harder than that. This, combined with the fact that Oded released all men from prison. Those who had been arrested and charged with gender-based violence were hunting down judges and the policewomen who put them behind bars. Those men were the ones to be feared more than the Balitan military.

He could still hear the high-pitched screams of the policewoman they had stoned in the square, along with a teacher who had been caught filtering homework packets to former students— girl students. She had staggered in a circle, mopping at the blood on her brow with one arm while reaching out to the spectators for help. Nasir had grabbed Jax's arm to keep him from assisting with so many of Oded's men surrounding her.

"Come. That woman's fate was set when the first stone was cast," Nasir had warned. *"Any interference from you will be your end and ours as well. It is fortunate that Alia has not met with the same."*

Nasir faced them and blinked rapidly, as though holding back tears of his own. Ajid, a place that once held so much promise with major advances for women and Zaras in every facet of life, was spiraling into darkness. The weight of it showed in the weary set of Nasir's shoulders.

One woman had backed away and disappeared into the continued assault of the mostly male crowd—men who were squarely aligned with Oded, but also unaware that first it would impact women and children. Then men who weren't wealthy would be the next targets. Obviously, Oded was taking a page from other political parties that aimed for a wealthy class and a serving class—nothing would exist between.

Jax's arrival had put a crimp in Oded's plans because they had fully expected him to ship out with the first wave of the Americans who left the country under strict orders.

At center court where the noise had risen to a deafening pitch, Jax had taken a final glance over his shoulder at the woman, then followed Nasir's advice and walked away. The screams echoed through his memory, but it was her eventual silence that unsettled his soul. That's when he knew he couldn't follow the American military's dictates and leave Alia here. He would do everything within his power . . .

Dro called Jax's name, snapping him back to the present. "I'm fully aware of what lies ahead," Jax admitted, closing the curtains, and shuttering the little sunlight making its way into the bedroom. "Which is why I'm trying so hard to get Alia out of here. Especially before one of her family members spill our little secret to the wrong person. Then it's game over. Thankfully, most extended family members had distanced themselves because it became apparent that Nasir's immediate family is one of Oded's main targets."

At one time, finding a quiet place to think, let alone talk, was damn near impossible with so many of Alia's relatives flowing in and out every minute of the day; but they had dwindled to a faithful few with every attack from the new regime.

He shifted on the bed and stretched out a little. "They've drained everyone's wealth in such record time that it also seems pre-planned."

Jax left the room and headed for the dining area—the epicenter of the household and the place Aunt Raja did her best knitting. The woman with a warm smile and big brown eyes, tossed Jax a twisted hank of knitting wool that he quickly untied and rolled into a ball—something that always made Alia laugh when he did, seeing him do something so simple. That sweet sound could bring a ray of sunshine to the darkest of rooms.

"There's more going on than you know." Jax's heart cramped in a mixture of wonder and fear at the reason this statement held true. "In a minute we'll have an even bigger problem."

"Bigger than what you already have?" Dro asked, the click of a turn signal echoing a little loud given the other sounds of traffic.

Jax let out a long, slow breath bracing for the blowback that was sure to follow his answer. "She's pregnant."

CHAPTER 3

"I'm surprised to see you here. Should I bring security?" Lamis Habib asked, while leaning on the door of Alia's former office. The agarwood scent he drowned in always greeted her before he even made it into the modestly furnished room. She cringed inwardly as it assaulted her senses.

Did the man eat the Aquilaria tree instead of bathing in its essence?

Her mouth filled with salt water when the man who was taking over her assignment flopped down in one of the chairs across from her desk, sending a plume of the noxious scent and sweat into the air. She was having a hard time keeping breakfast down. The little she was able to eat, despite Aunt Raja, a former nurse, encouraging her to take in more. She had been providing prenatal care as best she could since Alia certainly couldn't go to any doctors in the area. The few that didn't leave weeks ago.

When Lamis cleared his throat, she said, "No need to call anyone. I only came to retrieve the last of my personal effects. They are allowing us to at least do that."

Today, getting to the medical center was worlds easier than before. The throngs of people and the hustle and bustle had slowed to being almost nonexistent. So had the laughter of women, as men in dark suits or white robes talked quietly amongst themselves and watched for any infractions that would send innocent citizens carted off to prison. They had stared at the few women who moved about like ships on an ocean of sand and broken dreams, as they hurried to waiting cars with boxes of belongings in their arms. No one could have imagined things would become this bad, so fast. Nasir had to stay because his father had placed his name as power of attorney and the three granddaughters as beneficiaries of his estate. Until the case was decided, none of them could leave and their names were flagged at all checkpoints. They found that out the first time they tried to leave.

Rather than looking directly at her former colleague, Alia swiveled in her chair and carefully placed her parents' wedding photo in the box alongside her diploma and the awards she'd won for distinguished service. Those accomplishments angered quite a few people because she was new to the organization, and an American as well.

"I am sorry things turned out this way," he said fanning out his garment and circulating the stench.

"No, you're not," she snapped, pushing away from the desk. "You were the main one who campaigned to get me fired before they even offered me the position."

"That is not true," he protested, picking up her name plate, then buffing it with his sleeve. She gloated inwardly at the dark streak of dust it left behind on the crisp, white tunic. He grimaced and she tried not to chuckle. The act said so much. He was as tainted, lazy, and as unethical as they came.

"When I first came to the office, I received an email that someone sent to me by mistake without deleting the previous message string. You discredited every single one of my proposals to upgrade the staff training and facility by touting your limited experience over my American education."

She paused to let that sink in and he didn't deny it. He couldn't because everything she said was true. "Then you had several patients, along with your friends and family, send negative remarks to the medical board so that I would seem incompetent. Not once did you consider how unscrupulous that was." Alia reached across the desk and moved his hand from the box holding her clothes—ones she kept in the office in case of formal meetings. "You didn't take any courses to extend your knowledge base because you believed they would slide you into this position on gender alone."

Lamis put a vise grip on the glass award he held, and she gestured to his hand. Only then did he put it in the box with every-thing else.

Alia scanned the office, which was decorated in an array of warm colors, missing it already, as well as the people she worked with. She had only taken the position when the family's immedi-ately available funds had run out once the bureau froze the assets left by her grandfather and blocked any of the money coming from an American source. Everything was caught up in some fictitious estate lawsuit that was designed for the sole purpose of handing everything to Uncle Ibrahim who openly supported Oded and the illegal takeover.

"This is a career where you have to actually put in some work. You have to *know* things; how to anticipate process changes." She shrugged as though it didn't matter, but it truly did. She had made being in Ajid all this time work for her when the door leading for them to go back to America had mysteriously closed. "You'll see everything I'm telling you soon enough."

His olive complexion gained a slight red tinge as he absorbed her meaning.

With a smile, she added, "You may have book smarts, but your bedside manner and relationship with staff are sorely lacking. Oh wait, that's right. You don't have either one." She yanked open the top drawer and dumped the contents into her tote bag. The overflow went into a copy paper box next to it. She held onto one item for a moment.

"Is that company property?" Lamis asked, peering over the top of the box.

She turned the frame around to show an image of her two sisters, and he leaned in for a better look. A lustful glint lit in his eyes and Alia shuddered with disgust and quickly turned the photo over.

"My apologies," he said in a tone that belied his words. "You do understand, right? I mean, I had to ask because I heard your family has fallen on hard times." Lamis's eyebrows raised as a smirk teased the corners of his thin, wind-chapped lips. When his pasty tongue eased across that sandpaper smile, she swallowed hard as another wave of nausea washed over her.

Do you kiss your fiancée with that mouth? If so, she's going to need mouthwash with a hand sanitizer chaser.

She cleared her throat, cutting off a chuckle at the image that came with those thoughts. "We're facing some challenges, but we'll survive. I have every faith that my father will pull us through."

Lamis's countenance brightened as he moved to lean against the bookshelf. "If you were not already slated to marry Oded, I would have asked you myself."

She stood so fast, the picture frame slipped from her hand and clattered to the floor. "Where did you hear that?"

"He has put a severe warning out to everyone on the tribunal who matters," he answered with a dismissive wave.

"Warning?"

"That word is that you, your sisters, and nieces are off-limits to anyone except him and his family. Even the younger ones. What are their names again?" Lamis asked, squinting as though searching his memory but really was relishing the panic he hoped was setting in on her. "Don't tell me. It's on the tip of my tongue."

"Are you serious?" Alia sobered up as he continued his efforts to remember the names simply to taunt her. Everyone knew how protective their family was of each other.

The one and only time the four of them came to the hospital for a visit, her cousin, Lotus, hid behind Alia at the sight of Lamis, trying to avoid saying anything. Though she had been open and awestruck with everyone else she'd met that morning. Children could pick up on vibes better than adults.

"I do not like that man, Liyah," she had told Alia later as they ate ice cream at Sabra Nahir's. "His eyes lie. His words are false."

Alia studied Lamis as he attempted to smile, but the gesture looked painful and a little more than fake. The fine lines around his eyes crinkled. Lotus had clearly been right about him, but his assertion about Oded made sense and seemed truthful. She couldn't wait to share the information with Jax. The Farhats always had a fragile relationship with the Fadels. The jealousy existed because Oded's father had needed help from Nasir's father to start a business that failed, and he needed help again, and again. Nothing seemed to prosper so they instead blamed the Zaras as the reason they never succeeded.

"Are you sure you know nothing of this?" Lamis bit his lip and his grin widened as if that morsel of truth was the best bit of painful gossip he could impart.

"Thank you for the update." Alia deliberately chose her words for effect. Showing any kind of vulnerability in front of him was like dropping blood in shark-filled waters.

As if on cue, Lamis's fake smile dissolved into a sneer as he chewed on his bottom lip. His gaze crawled from Alia's face down to her breasts and paused for far longer than it should. She willed herself not to show any emotion at such a lascivious appraisal. Before now, doing such a thing could have landed him in prison.

"You know, if you do not want to be with him, all it will take is sharing my bed and you will become unavailable to him or anyone else," he offered in a lewdly suggestive tone. "I will bring you under my family's protection. We are politically connected. More than your uncle will ever be."

No thanks, I'm not into slime. Forget the hand sanitizer chaser. I'd probably need to bathe myself in the stuff.

"I'll pass," she chirped, not giving him the satisfaction of shielding herself.

"Oded has a reputation for —"

"Yes, I already know," she said, unwilling to let him put a voice to every woman's fears.

Aunt Raja had shared a story of a young woman Oded had tossed from his home without a stitch of clothing and not an ounce of dignity left. Some people on the street had stopped and stared. Others jeered and took pictures. Aunt Raja and four other women had circled the sobbing woman and blocked her from prying eyes while draping one of their pashminas to cover her nakedness. The woman's bruises told the story her mouth dared not speak. But with enough money, all of his indiscretions and atrocities were swept under the rug or disappeared. Power could do that. And now Oded Farhat had way too much of it.

Lamis leaned forward, still ogling her like a piece of freshly cooked lamb. "We would make a good team, you and me."

"I'll take my chances elsewhere," she shot back.

He winced at hearing those words. A hint of blood at the corner of his mouth made him look both comical and maniacal at the same time. "Elsewhere? On the last day of the American's evacuation, Oded is shutting off the internet, media, and all access to the outside world. You will have to give in to him—or me—at some point. You will not leave Ajid the same way your mother did."

"Who says I'm trying?" she asked, emptying another drawer into the copy paper box. Alia didn't have time to pack things properly. Nasir was waiting to escort her home. She could not be out in the street without a male family member, or she risked getting arrested again. She wouldn't see this side of prison bars again.

That fortunate mistake that meant she was released when over-crowding became a major issue, would not happen a second time.

"People talk," he warned, snatching the snow globe from her items, a reminder of her Chicago home. "Those shopkeepers in your district are not as discreet as you might think."

Alia shifted the contents in the box to make room for more. "What do you mean?"

"I am simply saying, you cannot trust everyone." He left his seat and inched closer, dropping the globe among her things. "Oded and his father has eyes and ears everywhere. Om Ali comes to mind."

"I'll take it under advisement." Alia dusted off her clothes and with it, any of the negative issues that he brought with him. But Om Ali, Oded's brother, falling from his lips was a concern. He was a huge part of the resistance. To his father's dismay, he had married a Zaras—one of the most outspoken women who raised a public voice against the atrocities committed against her people.

"Good, because you might not believe this, but I only have your best interest at heart. I always have." He reached for her, and she quickly moved out of range before he could make contact. "If you have some time, maybe you can show me how to—"

"Do the job you never wanted me to have?" she finished.

"I have just a few inquiries," Lamis insisted. His skin turned a delightful shade of crimson as he worked at sounding humble. That must have been painful. "I mean, what does it matter now? You do not work here any longer. It is not like I am asking you to—"

"Make *your* job easier?" She positioned both boxes and aimed to leave. "Surely you wouldn't ask *me*—a mere woman—of all people."

Lamis laid a hand on the top box, effectively trapping her in the enclosed space, and she froze.

Alia's father had taught her long ago how to handle schoolyard bullies. Meet them on their level, catch them off guard, then put a foot up any deserving rear end.

"You have told them that you are much more qualified than I ever was," she said, lowering her pitch to sound like him. "So, show them how wrong they were."

As she maneuvered around him, she stepped into the open area outside the office, her arm ached from wanting to knock Lamis on his tail in front of everyone who now had eyes on them.

"Do you not care about the patients?" he asked, following her movements.

"I will always care about them," she replied, relaxing her stance when it became clear that she wouldn't have to take him down. "As for this hospital, did they care when they surrendered to Oded's military even before the Americans' attempts to resolve the treaty issue? Did they care to make this neutral ground so everyone would receive medical care? Of course not. They saw a man in a tunic, complete with a spray-on tan, capped teeth, and appalling taste in cologne and put him in my place." She shivered for effect. "I am beyond fighting a battle they don't want me to win. Take care."

"You little—"

Alia scanned the faces of the remaining members of her staff, who had halted their movements to take in the exchange. She glanced over her shoulder, suddenly feeling like the weight of the world had fallen from them but didn't take away from the fact that she had so many challenges ahead.

One good thing had come out from this exchange. Her family had suspected Oded himself was behind the crusade to cause their downfall but could never connect the series of misfortunes. Now she knew for sure.

"Cheers to the man of the year that never was and never will be."

CHAPTER 4

"What in the entire—" Dro growled.

"It was *after* we tied the knot," Jax hurried to explain. "But people who aren't immediate family don't know that. They'll see that she's pregnant and won't know she's married and its perfectly fine for her to be that way. Virtue is bought and sold like precious oil around here. It'll be a major scandal—a public one. A deadly one."

Aunt Raja stroked a hand down her signature braid that nearly reached past her knee, then pointed to the window gesturing for him to close it on the next pass.

"The man aiming to marry her will say she's sullied, but because of this new not-quite-private campaign to have her, it will also be a huge embarrassment."

Dro was silent for several moments, but Jax knew those mental wheels were turning. "How did you manage to keep your wedding a secret?"

"Her father is an Imam," Jax answered with a half-smile. The entire wedding took about ten minutes and was the fastest one he had ever attended as an adult. The paperwork was quickly shifted through the proper channels by one of Nasir's few remaining friends. Om Ali's contact was able to get that new passport before the Balitan shut down that office.

"And no one else besides the immediate family knows?" Dro asked, possibly weighing whether it was worth his time and money to travel halfway around the world to help his wayward mentee.

And wayward was putting it mildly. In truth, Jax had been the worst student Dro had, but his mentor had held on to him even though he seemed to find fault in so much that Jax did. Yet, at some point, Dro took great pains to teach him, mold him, and test him.

More than once, Dro had taken Jax to task in front of a full room of grunts over a seemingly small infraction. The chastisement usually came after Jax had done something to help one of the weakest members of the team complete an assignment, but at the expense of not finishing himself. "They can't grow if you enable them," Dro said. "You have to become more adept at learning when the help is warranted and when self-preservation should kick in." With his stay in foster care, he'd been assisting others so long that it had become second nature. That part of him would never change.

Rumors began to fly in the rigorous, physical training sessions about Jax being the favorite or the golden child. Rather than battle the envious whispers or take it out on his teammates, Jax endured, focused on his studies, and quietly helped his classmates behind the scenes whenever the moment called for action.

The one and only time Jax ever stood up to his mentor, Dro apologized. The real or imagined excuses faded on Jax's part, and out of the dust rose a consummate soldier who finally stepped into his own and completed many dangerous missions. Dro had invited him to become a member of the Kings of the Castle's tactical team, committed to pay for his education as long as he stayed on a path far different than the tragic one his father had travelled.

The only people who clapped for him at the ceremony were

Dro and the teachers, because even years later his parents were still fighting their own demons and couldn't be bothered. Neither did any of the foster parents who had a hand in providing him a place to live and a few life lessons along with the experience.

"Earth to Jax. Do you read me?" Dro snapped. "I asked you how many people knew about the marriage."

Jax shifted his thoughts back to the current state of affairs. "We share a bed in a private area of the house when everyone else has retired for the night, but outside of that room and the house, we have to act like strangers. And it's killing me."

In truth, Alia was much better at hiding it than he was. When he craved her touch and forgot how they were supposed to act around others, she quickly pulled away. It actually hurt for her to ignore his gaze across a room filled with so many people. Every time Aunt Raja sat to rub Alia's back or feet swollen from standing for hours while filling in for her lazy sister, his heart hurt, and he felt that much smaller. Jax wanted to take care of her, be the one to brush her hair and breathe in that apricot-scented skin cream.

"Well, when you go for major issues, you go big," Dro teased with a little laugh.

"I never saw this coming," Jax admitted, rubbing his temples. "You of all people know what I went through growing up. Marriage was never part of my plan. But I did what I had to do. And I'd do it again—for her, a thousand times."

He scrubbed a hand down his freshly trimmed beard. "I figured I could spot her family some cash for a few weeks since the local authority is hitting them hard with all these bogus business fines and her arrest at the protests set them back a pretty penny. We couldn't allow her to stay in jail. We already knew the outcome if she did. But the persecution of this family has gone on longer than anyone could imagine ..."

Jax's words trailed off and settled on him like a weight. "She needed me, Dro. And what's worse is that they are putting the squeeze on us, I mean them. I mean ..." He shifted his focus on the stenciled Arabic emblems on the ceiling. "They are making it impossible for her to leave, and also impossible for the family to pay what they owe."

He could feel the family losing hope; could see it in the slope of Nasir's shoulders. The loss of Aunt Raja's laughter. The solemn expressions of Lotus and Fatima, who were fully aware something serious was going on, but didn't quite understand what. Amal, Simi, and Kamala seemed unaffected and that was another concern. The three of them would disappear from time to time, and Amal would slink around and listen in on conversations not meant for his little ears. *What were those three up to?*

"I've done what I could, but they've nearly depleted my first bank account. Since they realize an American is still involved, they're just milking me, believing I would come up empty at some point. When that didn't work as quickly, they found ways to block access to my other sources of funding. That's why I called you. We need cash and lots of it. And passports. Oded sent his men and the girls' passports were taken the first time Alia tried to leave."

Jax leaned against the window. He had hoped that the Kings could swoop in and handle this with their normal fanfare. He was proud to be affiliated with the Kings, Queens, and Knights.

Khalil Germaine, the founder of The Castle, built the organization for humanitarian purposes and had amassed a substantial amount of wealth and influence worldwide. When Khalil went on a five-year spiritual tour, it became overrun with dirty politicians, the Russian mafia, Mexican and Columbian Cartels, American crime lords, as well as local businessmen with their own sordid agendas.

The Kings of the Castle were formed to begin a series of dangerous missions that altered the path of their lives forever. They were powerful men, who were unexpectedly brought together by their pasts and current circumstances, and soon became a force to be reckoned with. So they, with all the connections at their disposal, certainly could make short work of the issue that Jax was dealing with, but they also knew when to fly under the radar. Level four travel advisories were no small thing.

"Alia needed me," he repeated in a whisper. "Never once has she asked for anything for herself. It's always about her family. Have they eaten? Is everyone safe? What can she do?"

"One chatter box is all you need," Dro warned, and the point was well-taken. "Though you're saying that the rest of the family stays away, someone's bound to figure it out and let it slip. Especially if jealousy is involved."

"You're right," Jaxon agreed. "The wrong words in the worst ears, then Alia will be exposed, and my neck will be on the chopping block right behind hers. We plan to end this by making a final plea for her case, the estate and for Simi and Kamala in front of the tribunal since we have to make another payment to them for Alia's fines, but as a Plan B, we need an out and there's not much we can do on our end. We need you."

CHAPTER 5

$\mathcal{T}$hirteen Days Before Evacuation

"HOW DARE you bring this foreigner into our chambers," Oded roared loud enough to echo throughout the tribunal hall, a massive brick structure that resembled the palace Oded and his family had also taken over. One of several that Malik Bakir's military failed to keep safe. The soldiers who were trained by several branches of the U.S. armed forces, claimed that American military left all of the equipment, but American contractors swept through the country and took all of the ammunition. Left guns, but no bullets. Left tanks, but no cartridges. Bakir's forces were easily overpowered. And the Balitan had wiped out not only the soldiers, but went after the families. His kind had never wanted Zaras or women to have a say in politics. No matter what the United Nations had decreed.

When it looked as though his military had faltered, Malik Bakir escaped with a jet filled with cash, gold, and diamonds, but left his wife and children behind. Somehow, he managed to take his younger fourth wife and her sister. The first, second and third wives were now imprisoned, and the daughters were given as "gifts" to high-ranking tribunal members who were amassing harems that rivaled those from centuries past.

The odd collection of men and women who catered to Oded's every need, stopped what they were doing, and a few guards left their outer post to move in and surround Jax and Nasir.

The two of them were facing down Oded in Tribunal Headquarters. The last stronghold that fell and ended the war before it truly began.

Surrounding palaces once served as a place where American leaders and world dignitaries would stay when slated to visit. Now they served as residences for tribunal members who reaped the benefits from being aligned with Oded.

Jax groaned inwardly, praying that none of the guards were bold enough to put a hand on him or his father-in-law. That would be the last time for them, but it would also mean he would have no hope of leaving Ajid, because he'd be in a cell and unable to protect his new family.

The air became tense and stifling. He calmed and centered his mind as others filed in; all of them aged and full of self-importance.

"You believe because the Americans are leaving that this country will suddenly spiral upward?" Nasir scanned the faces of the men who had taken their places among the semi-circle of seats. "Certainly not with the world imposing sanctions and your men taking the lion's share of the wealth while plunging us back into the dark ages."

"So, it is dark ages to follow scripture?" Oded countered as murmurs of discontent echoed from the rest of the men, most of them glaring at Jax because he represented the very thing they were aiming to break away from—American influence, American politics, and American lifestyles.

"You are blurring the intent of our religion," Nasir snapped.

"Law, Scriptures, and reinstating outdated tribunal traditions that only serve to make you rich are totally different things."

"This is not truly about religion, and you know it," Jax said, ignoring the grip Nasir placed on his arm. "This is about control and creating a state where men in power have no one to answer to, not even Allah." Jax moved closer to his father-in-law as Nasir's hands were now balled into fists by his side.

"You are mistaken," Oded said simply, taking in the fact that Jax was holding Nasir at bay.

Nasir chuckled, and the sound was as bitter as this exchange. He gave Jax's shoulder a comforting squeeze before turning towards the stone-faced members of the tribunal once more. "Am I? First taking away education for girls and then the women's work and taking their land, trying to wipe out an entire ethnic group. They are the ones who helped build this country and its economy when Malik Bakir was elected. They represented every-thing the United Nations had respected. It showed that we were a country that deserved a seat at the world table. Now, with what you have done, we are not even recognized by the United Nations until you make certain changes."

Discontent rippled through the men, their voices even louder than before.

"We will regain status again," Oded said with a smirk. "We do not need women or girls to do so. And we certainly do not need the Zaras, a bunch of mongrels of mixed blood."

"But you need their money, or you wouldn't be stripping everyone of all the value they have," Jax countered locking gazes with Oded. "And this economy has come to a standstill because of what you've done. The sanctions are telling you exactly how the world feels about what you have done. Women had already proved how valuable they are, but you and men like you are too blind to see it."

Some of the men stood, clearly offended as seen by their shocked expressions and raised voices.

"We are well within our rights to govern as we choose," Oded snarled, his face a mask of fury as he raised a hand to bring order once again. "You will see. My birthday is on the same day as the Americans' final day here. I will mark both with a celebration—a gala, concert, and leaders that are our allies, that will be televised for the world to see that we are well. This country will rise into the great nation it was before Malik Bakir tried to emulate and appease the west."

"What was so great about it before him?" Nasir roared, shaking a fist at Oded. "We were struggling to find our place among the world even then. With all of the massacres and human rights violations. Now you are hard-pressed to prove we are better than the West, that you would oppress both women and the Zaras—the life's blood of this nation. So that only a chosen few can flourish, and the rest become poor," Nasir said as despair and rage made his body tremble even more. "I am not seeing the same vision that Muhammad had when he valued women. When he united us under one faith. You are confusing culture for religion and that means you are wrong in this approach."

"Who are you to question what I do." Oded waggled a finger as if talking to a wayward child.

"This country cannot flourish if greed, corruption, and power have taken over the wealthy and the mindset of those who wield power," Nasir warned.

"You too, are wealthy. At least you were," Oded added with a smirk that didn't hide his pleasure at being the reason Nasir had hit a financial brick wall.

"How exactly did my status equate to yours?" Nasir shot back. "I did not massacre anyone to get mine. I did not lie or manipulate anyone. I live in integrity and honor. My personal wealth came because I listened to the wisdom of my wife. That is why my American portfolio is so expansive and why you believe that holding me and my daughters here in Ajid under false pretenses of settling the estate will give you access to it." He inhaled slowly and gave them a smile that caused a few to shift in their seats. "That will never happen. Everything is under my wife's control. I told you that I gave all power of attorney to her before I came here."

Oded's smile faded as he tried to rearrange himself in an ornate chair that resembled a throne. He tossed an angry glare at Ibrahim who quickly averted his gaze and seemed to wither under the weight of the unspoken accusation.

"Bring your wife here to Ajid," Oded commanded through his teeth. "I commanded all Ajidis and Zaras to return to Ajid. I demand that she return to save her husband."

"I love her too much to put her life in jeopardy again."

"Jeopardy?" Oded exclaimed, gripping the arm rests tightly. "We are not savages. Here, a wife supports her husband and if he calls to her, she is duty bound to respond and do as he demands."

"You, of all people, know why it has to be this way," Nasir said, scanning the faces in the room filled with men who were probably unaware that Oded had made subtle threats to have Siobhan as his own.

Oded laughed, but there was no joy in it. "I was not at all serious, and you know that."

"I could not take the chance then, and I certainly do not wish to do so now." Nasir smiled and shook his head. "Before, Zaras were promised safe passage, a safe return and then the next man to take power rescinded it. Thousands died believing this to be a better place. They are not so naïve any longer."

Oded flinched as the rest of the tribunal members seemed disturbed at Nasir's show of strength despite the heavy hand of fate squeezing the life out of his family. "If you do not comply, then your daughters will suffer until you do."

"My daughters are American citizens."

Oded was silent a moment as he scanned the expectant faces of everyone looking on. "Yes, but they are not in America right now, are they?"

Nasir turned to leave but was halted by Oded's parting words.

"Until your wife returns, your Visas, passports for your daughters to leave is denied. Your father's properties will all be confiscated and held in a public trust. The sanctions against Alia Fadel still need to be secured. They are now three times the amount. She was the most televised and human face of the resistance. The moment she is found in error again, she will be immediately retained as a repeat transgressor. And then Alia will be mine—I will marry her publicly and you will have no say in the matter."

CHAPTER 6

*a*lia walked into the house and straight into the spacious kitchen where the family took the majority of their meals these days. "I'm back Father."

"So, I see, and so early." He kissed Alia on both cheeks and smiled.

"What happened at the tribunal," she asked, and his gaze clouded over while Aunt Raja grimaced.

That can't be good.

"I would like to hear your good news first," he said.

Alia glanced at Aunt Raja who quickly averted her gaze so Alia would not see the tears that tried to form.

"Om Ali was able to sell off the last of the furniture and paintings to get us the cash we need." She opened her satchel and showed her father. "His exchange system and the secret paths he established to get the widows and their young children into Nadaum and later to Durabia, is like America's historical underground railroad." She slid the items his way. "Should I—"

He raised his hand and presented his palm. "Put it away for now. Give it to your husband for when we're ready to go."

Alia watched as her father moved around the open space and smiled taking the stool next to the kitchen sink. "I remember you slow dancing with Mama to Motown while spaghetti sauce simmered on the stove." Alia's voice sounded hollow in the kitchen as the weight of nostalgia filled the room. "Neither of you ever saw me. Mama's face lit up when she laughed at you trying to sing along with the words. I placed my hands over my mouth, keeping my laughter from escaping. You both looked so happy."

I can only hope to enjoy years of happiness with my husband.

Alia stroked the wedding band on her right hand. She normally wore it on a necklace that she kept close to her heart, but feared having it snatched since crime had also ramped up. Something in her father's expression crumbled.

"I don't regret coming here with you, Father. You know that right?"

Nasir worked at a response, then let his shoulders sag. "I was able to see my mother and father before they passed. But no one could have foreseen that our country would fall under this type of civil unrest, especially after so many advancements." He moved to the cabinet and retrieved several spices before returning to the counter where Alia stood, clearly waiting for her father to continue the history lesson.

"So yes, there are days my dear, my little habibti, that I do regret us coming back because of the danger you and your sisters are in."

"I often wonder if Uncle Ibrahim had something to do with the accident," Alia said. "The minute you arrived; he demanded new paperwork be signed giving him ownership of everything. He was trying to force the issue before you returned to America. I find that highly suspect. I truly believe he had them detain you because he didn't want you to leave before that transfer of assets happened."

Nasir busied himself with tying on an apron and washing his

hands to begin preparing their evening meal. Cooking always centered him; something he shared with his beloved.

"Why not just sign it over and be done?" Her voice was almost lost in the rush of the water splashing in the sink when Nasir turned the faucet off.

"My father's last words were actually 'do not let Ibrahim destroy our legacy. Do not let him consort with the Farhat family. It will be dangerous'." Nasir leaned against the edge of the sink. "He knew what the man was capable of, had watched some of the heinous things that he had done to people who defied him. It is no surprise that his own son is a mirror image."

Alia tried to stand, and her father raised his hand to halt her movements. "Rest child. Your grandfather never wanted Ibrahim to have anything to do with business. He knew that greedy and obsessive man had no discipline or ability to manage." Nasir snagged an apple, then rinsed it before peeling. He sliced it and placed it on a saucer in front of her. "Eat. You have been out too long, and you look weak around the eyes."

Rather than object, Alia complied. Her mouth filled with the sugary sweet texture, but her mind filled with all types of thoughts. She kept asking what else could go wrong.

Ultimately, despite the best laid plans something always did.

* * *

THE SOFT CHATTER of children singing and laughing came to Alia from the corner of the courtyard. As she looked at the wall on the other side of the compound, she smoothed a hand over her flat abdomen. She still remembered scrubbing the intricate blue tiling as a girl. The chore was her punishment for coloring in a religious book passed down from her father's people. She smiled as the arid breeze caught in the linen curtains that hung above, shielding her from the unforgiving rays of the winter sun.

The family compound was deceptively modest, by some standards. The lush pashminas adorning the walls and the architecture reminded her of something out of the fairytales she read as a girl. The images of flying carpets and Arabic soul music added a sultry soundtrack to the day and serenaded her to sleep at night.

"Are you in love with Jaxon Malone?"

Alia stroked the butter cream fabric of the chair she was seated in and frowned at the unwelcome intrusion. "Why do you ask, sister?"

Just as the sun rising in the east and setting in the west was a constant, so were Kamala's endless questions about Jaxon. *Does he like lamb? Is he a kind lover? Did he have siblings?*

In truth, it never dawned on Alia to ask those things. Jax's actions alone gave her security. It was as though he considered this marriage the real thing, not one of convenience. From the moment her father pronounced them as husband and wife, he made sure that she was never more than arm's length from him.

When they walked in the streets, he always moved her to the inside, using his own body as a protective barrier. He shared any meals or libations with her first. His tender care opened her heart, especially the night they were turned away from the airport. She was so afraid of what her fate would be. Jax stayed with her, and she pulled him into her arms. He resisted at first, but her need to be joined once again with him intimately was too great.

Kamala preened and posed in the doorway as though relishing the hot winds making her rich purple and gold dress flutter around her legs. "No reason," she quipped in a quirky voice that grated against Alia's nerves. "It's just that you're spending an awful lot of time with him. They say we had too much freedom in America, and I agree. The men should take care of us. Women don't need school or college or work. Just taking care of our husbands and children, nothing more."

Rather than take the bait, Alia moved into the sunroom overlooking the garden. The sandalwood oil her sister bathed in made her nauseous these days.

"No matter. My dowry will surpass needing book knowledge any day."

Alia bit down on her lip to suppress a chuckle. "What dowry, Kamala? Everything father had available is now tied up in America and thanks to Oded, our family's accounts are being drained each day."

Kamala tipped her chin in the air. "I will marry Oded and Simi will marry Nasir's younger brother. He loves me and not having a dowry won't matter."

Why all this dialogue about Oded?

Now Alia glanced at her reflection in the floor length mirror hanging on the wall. A wicked zing of satisfaction rippled through her body as she looked down at her midsection.

Before their extended family had abandoned them, she had been relegated to the dusty confines of an office and the library, keeping her out of the purview of the people Oded and his father sent by unannounced to "see to her well-being." Didn't matter. For all intents and purposes, she was fine, except for that little part of having to keep her love for Jaxon Malone a secret.

Alia returned to the room she shared with her husband. She picked up an article of Jax's clothes, sniffed it before tucking it into his suitcase. They were always prepared to leave on a moment's notice. She had feared for the time when the Balitan was totally in control. Then everyone would really suffer. She had done her part to protest, and it had cost her family dearly.

She could only pray that the protests around the world, and the sanctions placed by powerful nations, would help to create change. As it stood, suicide rates among Ajidi women had escalated to a dangerous point. It is different for those that didn't know what a taste of freedom was like.

For those who did, Oded Farhat was their worst enemy.

CHAPTER 7

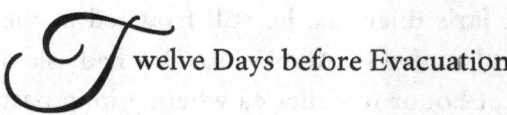welve Days before Evacuation

"I'M TAKING the next plane out to Ajid," Dro said, checking the breast pocket of his black blazer for his passport on the way to the mahogany desk that held a widescreen computer, a keyboard, and not much else.

Vikkas leaned back in one of the executive chairs on the opposite side and gave Dro an appraising look. "You know it's a hot zone over there. Everyone's trying to get out and you want to go in?"

"Jaxon has gotten himself into a bit of trouble," he replied, extracting money from the safe tucked behind an abstract painting by a local artist. He stacked the cash in an open briefcase along with the customs paperwork for the equipment he was bringing with him.

Dro took his time before meeting the taller man's inquisitive stare, barely remembering that since Vikkas was an international lawyer, he wasn't going to get away with such a short answer.

In truth, Dro planned to go alone, but the mere suggestion had sent Lola into a tizzy.

What if I lose you, too?

Lola wasn't exactly crying, but her quivering lips were his undoing. He'd sworn an oath to her as she slept in his arms one night. Hurting her was never an option, and while Lola knew what he did for a living, Dro still tried to keep any assignments he accepted on the right side of danger. She was strong and independent and had overcome the casualty of being the daughter of a prominent alderman in Chicago. Stability was what she longed for, and it was all Dro ever wanted to give her. He totally empathized when Jaxon said . . . *Alia needed me.*

While Dro understood Jax's dilemma, he still frowned at the situation the young man had landed in. All because Dro had asked him to escort Lola's maid of honor to America where a long past due family reunion, new position and the first Castle wedding of the year would take place.

"What kind of trouble are we talking about?" Vikkas asked, barreling into Dro's thoughts.

"The off-with-his-head kind," Dro answered, scanning the office and his mental checklist for anything else he might need, before turning to face his Castle brother once more. "The Farhat family, ones who were most feared in the region, are now basically the rulers of Ajid. They have a vendetta against Alia's family and escaping is going to be damn near impossible."

After a moment of reflection, he filled Vikkas in on a few more details. When he was done, Vikkas let out a low whistle of amazement.

"Thought Jax had plans to be the last single man swinging from vine to vine on the planet," Vikkas teased with a comedic lift of his eyebrows.

Dro shook his head and tried not to smile but failed. The timing wasn't the best and neither were the circumstances. Deep down, Dro was thrilled Jax had settled down like so many of the men within The Castle ranks. Jax was the only one who talked a good game when it came to avoiding love and relationships, but his actions didn't quite match his words. Jax's deep respect for women, and heart space for children were unlikely soft spots considering the type of work he did and the missions The Castle sent him to complete.

Dro had laid eyes on Jaxon Malone again a few years after keeping the promise he made at graduation. The younger man was playing soccer with some of the local children near the Gaza strip during a recovery mission. While the other men were coming up empty in door-to-door searches for information on the criminal they sought, Jax shared his rations with the children. He had asked all of the men in the unit to give up their rations and some money so he could hand it over to the families of the children who had secretly helped them.

By nightfall, Jax had the coordinates to the safe house and the place where four women and three girls were being held hostage. Jax had a unique way of using empathy and making connections to make short work of long days. The mission could have lasted several months, instead of two weeks if Jax had not secured that valuable intel. His request was a small sacrifice compared to going home to be with family months earlier than anticipated.

"Yes, I can see why that would be a major issue," Vikkas said glancing at the large sums of cash stacking up. "Didn't he realize that they don't play over there when it comes to their women? Especially with American men? And Zaras are the most persecuted ethnic group in that area?"

"He was thinking with his heart instead of his head." Dro tossed in the last of his paperwork while still remembering the quiet conviction in Jaxon's voice. Those three words moved him like no other. *Alia needed me.*

"Heart?! That's not *all* he was thinking with." Vikkas chuckled while covering his eyes with a hand.

"Watch it, Vikkas," Dro growled. "Someone could make the same statement about you when you stumbled back into a certain lady's life." He gave a death stare that made Vikkas squirm. "You would've taken on the devil himself just to keep her safe. Which head were *you* thinking with when she was in the thick of things, ready to die to protect us. Or when she put that bullet in her brother for trying to take things too far?"

Vikkas sobered instantly. "Point taken. I apologize. His timing could use a little work though. I'm just saying."

Dro threw up his hands in mock surrender and backed off, knowing Vikkas was right. "Jax is only doing what any man worth his salt would do. Protecting his new family is job one. Especially since his bio family was so tragic. That's the kind of men we want as part of The Castle. What's done is done. He married her, though it still won't save them from being stoned when she starts show-ing." Dro ran a hand through his hair and tried to ignore the shudder of unease coursing through him. The kind that normally came before a storm. And what Jax had set in motion was a major one.

"Start showing?" Vikkas, who was normally more composed, showed complete shock when his mouth fell open and he sat ramrod straight. "Wait, are you saying she's pregnant too?"

Dro grimaced and wanted to kick himself for that slip. "Yes, I kinda left out that part."

"You think?"

"Well, I leave in a few minutes to handle things over there," Dro said, dismissing the sarcasm. "I needed to make an overseas trip anyway because the rings are being custom made by Sydney Lomax, another friend of Lola's. That's as a surprise, but she's receiving an award there and it makes sense for me to handle that business. Along with a few other non-negotiables for this wedding." He snapped the briefcase shut. "So, I'll pop over, spread the right amount of money in the right hands, get Jaxon and Alia, connect with Michelle DaCosta for the dress, Valentina Romano about the cuisine, and Noelle Jakob about importing the flowers, then swing by Durabia to pick up the rings right after. And all will be well."

"'All will be well' are famous last words. When have things ever gone according to plan with you?" Vikkas asked, giving him an intense look as he leaned against the chair he'd just vacated.

The concern in Vikkas' eyes was disturbing and understandable, but for Dro there was no other way forward. He had to get Jax and Alia out of that place because the things he'd been hearing on that side of the world since Oded Farhat had seized power, were alarming.

The deadly weight of the Desert Eagle in his shoulder holster shifted against his side. "I just need to stop by Martina's office and snatch up the passports she's making for Alia on a rush basis. And bring enough cash. That's always what makes problems go away in that area."

"And you're taking a Durabian passport for yourself, Jax and you'll get one for Alia, just in case, right?"

"Not necessary. We have American ones," he said, tapping the gold seal on his passport. "All we have to do is have one of Om Ali's connections get the Visa, then make it to the American military base and we're good. I'll see you in a week."

Vikkas moved until he was mere inches from Dro, blocking his path. "And where the hell do you think you're going without back up?"

Dro froze, inched backward, and smiled. "Evidently, nowhere."

CHAPTER 8

*A*lia covered her hair and could barely move in the dark weighted material. The heat was stifling tonight, but even more so because she couldn't wear material that would allow her skin to breathe. This dress code enforcement was nearly absolute and swift because men would suffer for any infraction of their wives and children. Severe punishments and prison time awaited.

Now she was a nameless, faceless being the Balitan desired all women to be. Kamala risked imprisonment again and the exorbitant fees or worse that came with it just by being out without an escort. Alia had to know why she continued to disappear despite father's repeated warnings.

She kept to the shadows as much as possible. The streets leading to Oded's lavish palace were nearly empty. The few other women walking nearby with their husbands were dressed mostly the same with no way to know who was friend or foe.

The lesson was swiftly brought home due to emptier pockets which meant curfews and codes were now fully respected. But not Alia. Not tonight. She mirrored Kamala's movements, wondering why her sister felt so emboldened to walk without looking over her shoulder or without an escort as if she had no fear of consequences. Guards allowed her to pass without question; while Alia was forced to duck behind houses and trees to obscure her presence.

She watched Kamala sail through the palace entrance with ease. The guards didn't give her a second glance. Alia kept her body against the stone and slid toward the back of the house hoping to figure out where Kamala would end up. She froze a few feet outside the rear window of Oded's palace compound when she heard that familiar voice.

"You will keep your promise that I will be taken care of?"

"Of course, Kamala," Oded replied smoothly and even Alia could tell it was a lie. The man had no truth in him whatsoever, but her naïve little sister would never understand that.

"Our families are so close," he continued. "I do not understand why your father wants Alia to be with someone else. Maybe that American living with you who has thwarted my plans? She will belong to me, just as you will."

Kamala gasped. "Why do you need her if I am willing to publicly marry you because you want a Zara wife?"

The silence stretched between them. Kamala, with her usual impatience, rushed to fill it. "I asked, why do you need her if I am willing to do whatever you want? I'm even betraying my father and family to do so."

My word, it isn't just Uncle Ibrahim.

A quick chat with her sister's friends, only served to spark a desire to follow this particular sister because none of them knew her comings and goings. She had lied, she was not with Maya as she had led father to believe. She had been making tracks to Oded's and securing her position as first wife to the leader of the new regime. So selfish. And equally dangerous. In the silence, Alia knew he was already formulating something to placate Kamala.

The soft breeze eased the curtain aside just enough for Alia to catch Oded's movement as he rounded the glass table. Kamala shielded her face momentarily, then squared her shoulders in a feeble attempt at defiance or to absorb the blow she thought would come.

"You are *nothing* like your sister," he spat. "That intelligence. That fire. The steel in her spine ..." He sighed with the kind of appreciation that made Alia's skin crawl. "It would be my great pleasure to break her. You are already broken, so there is no pleasure in being with you."

"But at least I am a virgin. Intact."

"I do not mean that kind of broken," he said and the contempt in his voice was not hard to miss. He lowered his hand and stormed away.

"My sister might not be," she taunted, and her voice was much stronger. "She is very close with the American . . . Jaxon Malone. Maybe ... too close."

Oded whipped around to face her and quickly crossed the distance between them again. "Are you certain?"

Alia braced herself against the pain this level of betrayal brought. She should have been watching Kamala more closely all along. When the girl stopped complaining so much, that was a sure sign that something else was going on. Alia had been too preoccupied to put it all together.

Kamala was a spoiled, pampered princess who hated school studies and household chores. She spent more time on social media and video chats, parties with friends and being with the wealthy families in the area. All empty pursuits and something she didn't realize would no longer be open to her when the new regime made good on its threat to close off the internet, media, and access to the outside world.

"Iron sharpens iron, and I will sharpen Alia Fadel until there is nothing left," he warned. "You, on the other hand, are pliable like cheap metal. A harsh word or hand will set you to rights soon enough." He reared back as if to strike. She flinched and he grinned. "Never question my methods again. The agreement was always that our families would combine. I never said you would be favored."

"Papa said there wasn't any type of agreement. That was never in writing," she countered, venturing a glance over her shoulder as though she sensed someone.

Alia inched back a little.

"Did it have to be?" he roared with a fist waving near her face. "Your family has always thought that they were better than everyone else. Now they are not so different than the rest of the Zaras, are they?"

Oded's smile was nothing short of frightening. *Why can't she see how evil he is?*

"With every obstacle, your father will learn that you all are more like commoners, despite the American success. You're still a lowly Zaras. I will have you, and her, and the younger ones will be given as gifts to the members of the tribunal who desire them. Possibly my father."

Kamala's hand flew to her chest. "You said they would be given in marriage to the sons of tribunal members, not gifts."

"A bunch of mongrels?" he snarled. "Certainly not. I said they would be provided for. Marriage is out of the question for them." Oded wrinkled his nose in disgust as he returned to his seat behind the ornate desk as though Kamala's nearness unsettled him.

The real reason, one he had not shared with Kamala, was that Lotus and Fatima were not rich, nor did they have any American ties to wealth or land as Alia, Kamala, and Simi did. Lotus and Fatima were pure Ajidis since grandfather's first wife was Ajidi. Nasir's mother was Zaras, and that bloodline carried to his daughters.

"That is not what was promised if I helped you," Kamala protested as tears streamed down her face. "It was to be first wife and—"

"Are you contradicting me again?" he growled, shaking a finger in her direction. Whatever expression he wore made Kamala back away several feet.

"Have you forgotten your place, already?" He dismissed her with a wave. "Maybe you will not make such a good second, or even third wife after all. Maybe a concubine, but not a wife."

She dropped to her knees, clasping her hands in a beseeching manner. "Oh no, please, please forgive me. It is just that I want what's best for them."

"Are you quite certain of that?" His laughter echoed off the walls and carried through the courtyard. "You only asked about their security *after* you had sought out comfort and the best position for yourself." He folded his hands across his paunch of a stomach. Too much excess had made him take on a different shape—less athletic. "Spare me this late concern for your sisters and cousins. You only now realized how this will look when they find out you are the reason they have met with so many challenges. You are the reason that they will be nothing more than servants and a source of pleasure. Unlike Ibrahim, your information has proven more valuable since that troublesome American arrived."

Oded left the desk and paced the area in front of the shelves of antique books, ones Alia was certain he had not read—only book he took stock in was scripture—ones used to bolster his warped ideology. "Their money has found its way into my private accounts. Most of it right here in the safe since the banks are unstable," he said, wrapping his knuckles against the door of a cabinet right behind him. "I have you to thank for that. Like all loyal pets, I will reward you handsomely. I just haven't said how."

A door opened off to Alia's left and she quickly ducked behind a huge plant. Several women, dressed in the same insufferably hot coverings, made their way down the passage that led to another row of palaces. A group of men followed, carrying on a lively conversation while the wives remained silent. Again, so different than a few months ago—when everyone seemed happier, and women had a voice and a choice.

A mixture of rage and sadness filled her heart as she abandoned her place at the window and aimed to make it home. She could not tell her father what she had found out about Kamala. It would break his heart. And she couldn't say *how* she found out because she was not supposed to be out unescorted as well. Dro and Vikkas were set to arrive in the morning and the dynamics would shift. She had to figure out a way with Aunt Raja to get a handle on Kamala.

She was nearly at the gate before realizing that since Kamala had not come out. She might still be in danger from Oded's wrath because she did not know how to temper her words. As much as her sister deserved whatever Oded doled out, Alia also couldn't abandon her. She doubled back and returned to spy on the sister who had betrayed them in such a foul manner.

This time, she acted as if she was tending to the flower and plants outside the window and stole a peek at the two inside.

"Do you at least promise not to harm my father or Aunt Raja?" Kamala asked in a trembling voice, making Alia wonder what had transpired in those few moments she was away.

"Now, that is out of my hands," Oded admitted with a devious glint in his eyes. "They are Zara and tribunal will decide their fate. The American is a different story. We will use him to force the return of our captives who are being held in American prisons."

Kamala shook her head. "I don't think that is the way it works with the United States. They do not negotiate with terrorists."

"Who said anything about terrorists?" he snapped, causing her to inch backward. "This will be a simple exchange; that is all. And what would you know about any of this? Keep your head out of men's affairs." He moved forward, pushed a finger into Kamala's chest and it took everything in Alia not to charge in and flatten him. "You are a perfect example of why girls should not be educated beyond fourth grade. You know too much."

"Fourth grade?" She tossed back. "That is barely enough to read."

"Exactly," he said, raising a victory fist before moving to the desk. "Be able to read scripture but should only know what your husbands tell you and nothing more."

"Some of us already have a university education," she countered, and it sounded strange to hear her sister defend women being educated since Kamala did not enjoy school in any way— except the social aspects.

"And those will be the first to be broken," he said, pushing an empty glass to the side next to a bottle of bourbon, a drink that was forbidden in Ajid. "We will do it publicly so there are no misunderstandings about the fact that the old traditions will be strictly enforced."

Somehow more brave than she should be in the face of such adversity, Kamala asked, "And when the world sanctions this country the same way they did Afghanistan, we will all suffer because of it."

Oded shrugged, affecting an air of nonchalance. "We will produce everything we need here to sustain us. No outsiders should tell us how to run our country."

Kamala shifted to a more comfortable stance; her chin titled upward. "And evidently you do not understand exactly how much international trade drives this economy," she countered, and her voice held a note of pride at enlightening him; a man who should already be well aware of these things. "With trade drying up from Europe, Great Britain, America and Durabia, this country is already at forty-nine percent poverty level. You are going to make us into a country that is ninety percent poverty." She could barely contain her laughter as she added, "Yes, that will show the world *exactly* how powerful we are."

Oded came to Kamala's side in a move so fast that if Alia had blinked, she would have missed it. She offered up a silent prayer for her sister's safety and a hope that her outright laughter had not bruised his fragile ego.

"If I did not believe it would cause too many inquiries," he growled, "I would slap you hard enough for you to realize your error."

"My error? In speaking the truth?" she asked, and her tone did not hold an ounce of fear. That was dangerous in and of itself. "Trust me, America will broadcast your mistakes for the entire world to see. The Americans stirred things up with the United Nations because the tribunal broke their word about fair treatment of us."

"The previous regime signed that treaty. We do not have to honor it. The Zaras should not exist," he said with yet another dismissive wave as though she was some pesky insect. "You speak too much. Make sure your family is at the celebration. Now leave this minute. Out of the back entrance, and make sure no one sees you."

Alia's heart did an anxious pitter-patter in her chest while figuring out her next move. In trying to make herself seem more knowledgeable, Kamala had actually spit out what she'd been overhearing in their household discussions with Jax. Knowing all of this, why would she side with Oded against her family this way? Was she so adverse to school and goals?

"After everything I've done for you, I have to sneak out like a thief?" She whined in a petulant tone. "After all, I am fully covered right? What will give me away? My eyelashes?"

Good grief. Are you trying to get yourself killed, Kamala? This man is responsible for the death of thousands of our people.

Kamala paused at the door and glanced over her shoulder, possibly believing she was far enough out of his reach. "Do you know who these new laws are really protecting us from? Your precious men, who can't seem to exist unless women are invisible. Men who also can't control their sexual urges or their need to beat women until they can't be recognized. That certainly hadn't been the case under Malik Bakir. So maybe they should be the ones to cover up and have blinders on. Maybe they are the ones who need restrictions."

With that, she swept from the room leaving a red-faced Oded to ponder her words.

CHAPTER 9

$\mathcal{E}$leven Days Before Evacuation

"YOU MUST TURN around and go back," the bald portly guard said, while rocking on the balls of his feet as though speaking those words brought him some level of satisfaction. His shoes were covered with dust, though he was inside the pristine confines of the airport terminal that was only one-hundred yards from the American military hangar and base. Evidently, he had travelled from an outlying checkpoint to work and failed to tidy up before taking position at his current space.

He checked a screen, narrowed his gaze, and handed back their passports but tore Alia's in half before they could stop him. "She is not allowed to leave Ajid."

Dro and Vikkas had arrived an hour ago, met Alia, Jax, and Nasir at the airport's checkpoint with the cash to pay Alia's fines and leave some currency with the rest of the family. Some was secretly earmarked for Om Ali to continue his work of getting the policewomen, judges, military women and other targeted Zaras out of the country.

"We are American citizens," Jax insisted, as Dro put a warning grip on his arm making him look up in time to see several American soldiers come closer to watch the exchange.

Vikkas said, "According to the terms of engagement with the United States, you can't detain us without a specific reason—a *criminal* one."

Sweat made the officer's khaki uniform shirt cling to his barrel of a chest. A pair of beady dark-brown eyes drifted over Jax, Nasir, and Dro, before settling on Alia, who was hidden in the yards of black fabric that made up her new burka. "We can always create one," the man said with a sneer as another, much shorter guard, joined him. "But we do not have to. She has charges pending and will need a *special* visa to leave Ajid. That is part of the new terms. *She* cannot leave. Neither can he," the guard gestured to Jax. "Because he signed the paperwork to secure her bond until her case goes before the tribunal again. That will not happen until after the Freedom Celebration and all of those meddling Americans are gone."

"Say the word," one of the American soldiers said, as more of them moved in to overtake the two guards blocking their progress.

Dro held up a hand to keep them at bay. They could offer an armed show of power, but the country was too unstable and it could affect other Americans who were still within the country trying to make it out before the deadline. Jax, Dro, and Alia could also make a run for it, but Oded's military had no problem putting a bullet in people who didn't necessarily deserve it.

"Turn back, or we will arrest you and have every reason in the world to do so." He grimaced as he handed the passports back to them and saw the emblem of the one on top.

"He can leave," he said, gesturing to Vikkas who was already past the checkpoint and among the hordes of people striving days ahead of the official end date. Then he looked at Dro and said, "He can as well, but the rest cannot."

Jax moved in to say more, but Nasir gripped his shoulder. The older man's ancient hazel eyes silently pleading with him to back down reminded Jax of Alia's. Jax caught a glimpse of Vikkas pocketing his Durabia passport as he came back to stand on the Ajid side of the area. Evidently, he had made it through the checkpoint because his passport showed he was a citizen of Durabia, not the United States. Durabian passports wouldn't receive the same scrutiny as American ones. And even then, Ajid did not want any smoke from Durabia. Even if their names were flagged, the guards wouldn't hold them back. Durabia was the only reason why food and care packages were making it into Ajid. They were earmarked for Zaras, but a good deal of it landed in Ajidi hands.

Maybe they could have some smuggled in. Hopefully, they would arrive before the celebration.

The group wound their way through the packed terminal, walked outside toward Nasir's vehicle in the multi-level parking lot. Vikkas scanned their faces. "Criminal charges? Someone want to clue me in?" he asked, opening the door, and signaling for Nasir to make room for him.

"This is something different," Jax said. "First, they wouldn't let Alia leave, but I could leave. Now they are not allowing *any* of us to leave except you two. Even with Nasir here to vouch for us and provide paperwork for the marriage and Alia's new last name. I was so hoping that we'd be on the American base and in the air by the time they figured out that she was still a wanted woman. They must have us on some kind of watchlist for Americans."

"Or they put notes into the computer the last time we tried."

Alia leaned into Jax's chest and closed her eyes, struggling to hold back tears. Nasir lowered his gaze to the ground as his shoulders bowed in defeat. Somehow Dro's plan of taking a puddle jumper from the American base to Cairo, then a flight to Durabia faded in the wavy shimmering heat of the day.

"My biggest question is how did they know she was Zara when her passport clearly says American."

"Zaras are an ethnic blend of Persian, Iranian, Mongolic, Turkish, and Asian," Jax said. "They have a distinct look that distinguishes them from the Ajidi features which are more Middle Eastern and East Indian which is the blended base of their cultures. They can look at her, Nasir, and her sisters, and tell."

"The faith was supposed to unite us," Alia said. "But they use ethnicity and culture to divide us."

Vikkas and Dro shared a glance and they absorbed everything that Jax had hoped not to impart in front of Alia and her father. All of it was too painful given how many people who had been massacred for being of a different ethnicity, even though the faith was supposed to make them one.

"Alright, evidently, we don't know the full story, can you all fill us in?" Vikkas said as Dro nodded and gestured for Jax to remain silent as Nasir and Alia shared what was going on. When they were done covering the tragic history of the Zaras who have been the target of ethnic cleansing; they moved on to America's involvement in encouraging Zaras and women to take part in the war. Followed by the fact they abandoned those same women when they needed to leave the country, and how Alia became the public voice of Zaras who had been mistreated and the ones who were used to make an example.

Jax slammed his fist on the dashboard, causing everyone to flinch. He tried hard not to curse. "They said if we made it to the American military base, we'd be home free."

"It's more than that," Vikkas said, taking off his blazer. "I analyzed everything you've been saying this past week, Before Nasir left the states, he made sure that only his wife had complete control. Now it seems like they're upset that Nasir doesn't have access to the funds in his American portfolio and want her to return." He looked over to Nasir and patted him on his back. "She's well aware of what's happening here. They blocked Nasir's phone.

Through Om Ali's connections, Nasir was able to get a final communication to her not to get on a plane and come back to Ajid; no matter what demands from the new government were sent her way. She hasn't left the safety of home despite several personal missives from Ibrahim saying that Nasir and Alia were in trouble and need her."

Dro put his focus on Alia. "So, let me get this straight, they're pilfering her grandfather's estate, forcing Nasir's hand and leaving him no choice but to marry off his daughters." Jax met Nasir's gaze in the rearview mirror; the fear in his eyes was well-founded. "If he doesn't consent, then they might take drastic measures. Then his daughters will have no chance to land anywhere as wives, they will be servants with no rights or protections whatsoever."

"Indentured servitude?" Dro and Vikkas asked in unison, and the anxious expression on Nasir's face matched exactly how Jax felt.

"Until the family's debts are paid. Even though those debts are manufactured, and they will keep adding more onto Alia's fines to make sure she will never be free."

"That sounds more like ... slavery." Vikkas grimaced, angling to face Nasir. "In this day and age?"

Jax knew this one fear kept the older man up most nights, pacing to the early hours of the morning.

"It still exists everywhere in the world, but here, it is more horrific," Nasir said, his tone solemn and foreboding. "Unscrupulous men make the rules. People like us are left at a disadvantage because we are weighted down with laws steeped in man's twisted interpretation blending tradition and religion."

"Why didn't the girls leave with your wife," Dro asked Nasir.

"Because his father named them as beneficiaries," Vikkas answered for them. "They wouldn't be allowed to leave until the estate has been decided."

Dro's eagle-eyed gaze swept the area, and he gestured forward with his head. "Drive. We aren't safe sitting here this long. If someone reports what we tried to do, they might send someone to pull us in."

Nasir pulled into traffic.

'Sounds like under this new regime, having Nasir's daughters cast into that type of service would be a fate worse than death," Vikkas said, and raised his gaze to the ceiling before closing them completely.

Jax placed his hand on the old man's shoulder as a chill settled in the car. Everyone took his deadly meaning. "It won't come to that. We won't let it." He studied a nest of policemen standing several feet away who were watching dozens of female protestors who were squaring off against them. The policeman did not make a move against them because the American military were also watching. Oded had not been truthful about the fact that he imprisoned the opposition or Zaras, so these women might be safe now, but Jax prayed for their safety if the police were taking note of who participated and hunted them later.

"Look at that. Not one man protesting on the women's behalf?" Alia scoffed, then tore her gaze away as she shook her head. "The men are all right with allowing this because they want complete control again. Even if it comes at the expense of their happiness or the fact that they don't realize that it will only benefit men in power."

Dro and Vikkas shared a glance.

"So, we'll need to check into a hotel and then let's focus on the next steps," Dro said cutting through the sad vibes before hopelessness took hold again.

Jax recognized the obvious effort at distraction by focusing on solutions instead of lamenting the problems.

"You can stay with us."

"We know that, and we thank you," Dro said. "But we need to establish a place away from your home because it's being hotly watched right now. And we're able to have money wired in at the hotel if it becomes necessary."

"That's if the banks will allow it," Jax said. "There are restrictions on international banking. And the economy is collapsing."

Vikkas flipped open his passport, and stroked the emblem embossed on the purple leather cover. "We have to get Durabian passports brought in for everyone. Are there any other ways of leaving the country that don't involve the airport, military base, or main routes?"

Nasir turned back to the conversation with a sad smile. "Yes, but they're so dangerous that we might as well accept our fate and stay put. Better to be alive and have hope, than buried and hopeless."

"That doesn't sound good." Vikkas looked at Jax then peered in the rearview mirror as the airport faded out of view. "There's always the water."

"We checked into that." Jax stroked a hand across Alia's cheek as she slept peacefully even with all of the chaos around them. Their baby and worries about their future constantly kept her up at night. "They patrol that area more than any others because of the amount of trade coming in from Durabia, Nadaum, Afghanistan, Saudi Arabia, and India. Millions of dollars worth of goods pass through that way. And with American and European sanctions settling in, they're going to need it."

"But that means their attention is on the surface, not the deep parts," Vikkas countered, tucking his passport away.

"Are you thinking what I'm thinking?" Dro turned in his seat, wearing a huge grin despite the seriousness of the moment.

"If I was thinking what you're thinking, I'd be making a whole lot more money."

Dro's smile faded as his eyes took on that intense look that always made Jax dread what came next. "I need you to be serious right now."

"Have to keep it light or the sadness will swallow us whole," Jax said, flickering a gaze between his Castle brothers and Nasir.

"You know my golden rule, right?"

Jax grimaced and tried to keep his voice level. "Say yes and figure it out. I always hated that saying because it usually involves everyone being thrown in the deep end of things and trying to climb to safety with your ass barely intact."

"The water at night is going to be our best way out," Vikkas said, his gaze sweeping across the mansions with acres of lush greenery between them.

"One other problem, you all haven't considered, though," Jax said.

Dro's gaze locked on Jax as he asked, "What's that?"

"Alia's deathly afraid of large bodies of water."

All hope of another way out dissipated as fast as Vikkas had come up with the idea.

"And that's beside the fact that she can't swim."

CHAPTER 10

D ro's head went back as he groaned with frustration. "That's definitely a problem. We'll need to come up with a strategy to combat that. Vikkas is going to work on getting those passports to a safe place where we can retrieve them. Om Ali can help with that. But I think that the water route is our only way out of here."

"The guards are going to stop us at the airport each and every time and the military can't do much about it," Alia whispered.

"We've already tested everything else," Jax told them. "Air and ground are out of the question."

"But that's going to be a whole lot to maneuver. And here's another issue. We might have to get everyone out at once. We can't just slide Alia out of here and leave the rest of the girls." Jax took Alia's hand in his. "Oded and his father will be angry enough to have one of them take her place. And with their newfound power, and no outside media watching, he will not be gentle about it."

"So, we're talking four additional?" Dro surmised.

"And two of them are Ibrahim's daughters," Vikkas said, putting his focus on Nasir. "We have no right to take them. We have some time for them. They should be safe, right? Aren't they all underage?"

"If they are taken by Oded, their age will not matter," Nasir responded. "And the proper protections for marriage will not be in place. Ibrahim does not have their best interest in mind given how their mother left him."

"I mean, why not the whole family?" Vikkas asked, sounding a bit sarcastic. "The more the merrier. Hell, we can be like the Von Trapp family." When Nasir frowned, he added, "That family from The Sound of Music? Anyone know that song they croon about the female deer? Maybe singing will get all of us across because this is not the kind of plan that'll keep everyone alive and can land us all in custody."

"He's right, it's too risky," Dro admitted. "The more people we add, the more likely it is that we'll be caught. Someone will have to stay behind. Then we'll have to make a second sweep to get the rest."

Streams of cars in the opposite direction were piled up with people trying to make it out through the airport since the majority of outlying checkpoints had been shut down and became military posts. How many of them would also be turned away?

"Say yes and just figure it out." Jax placed a hand on Dro's shoulder. "That's basic stuff, man. You taught me that, or don't you remember? We're not leaving anyone."

As the vehicle traveled into the Demeira area, industrial buildings remained as silent as the women who used to work there making money to feed their families.

"Aunt Raja is widowed, she'll be safe?" Dro asked as Nasir swept past the restaurant district and slowed near one of several that the family owned; one that had been closed for three months under falsely made-up violations. Along with others.

"Relatively," Jax whispered.

Vikkas frowned as his brow furrowed. "Why not definitely?"

"If the money runs out, and the girls are not able to satisfy the required amounts for the debt or his desire for a public Zaras wedding, they might turn to whoever is available," Nasir reasoned, and his tone was grim. "Even a widow. There is a method to their thought process. Women have more value as ... servants. Women do physical work daily, take care of sexual needs at night, and give birth to more property. Men, in turn only serve one purpose—work."

"But we don't want anything to happen to any members of our family either." Jax glanced out of the window and pointed at the bridge walk nearby. "Stop the car."

Nasir drove a few more yards before Jax shoved the door open, causing him to stomp on the brakes, forcing the cars behind them to come to an abrupt halt. He eased the car onto the shoulder as Jax walked over to the bridge and looked at the water flowing through a man-made channel.

Dro and Vikkas were right behind him. "And throwing yourself into traffic helps us how?" He nudged Jax in the side. "People could've gotten hurt just now because you're a red ball of emotion. You needed help and we're here. Don't fold on us. Use your words. Tell us what's really going on with you."

Traffic picked up again and echoes of chatter reached where they stood.

"Hannah was three. Sophie..." He took a moment to collect himself. "Was nine," Jax said, closing his eyes and releasing a weary sigh.

Dro moved close as a couple scurried past them giving them a curious look.

Jax stared at the water again, longing to be sitting at home in Alia's presence, listening to her sweet voice, and inhaling her beautiful scent. At least, if he were alone with her, the world would cease howling. With Alia, the world just stopped, and he could breathe. With everything he had been through, no one else provided such a sense of calm, direction, and safety. He could not fail her. He could not fail this family.

Out of the corner of his eye, Jax caught a glimpse of Dro folding his arms as he leaned against the railing with his back to the water. Nasir left the car and Alia was walking towards them. With a nod from Dro, Nasir placed a hand on her shoulder to halt her movements to give them space.

"You know, I was in and out of foster care as a kid," he said, choosing his words carefully.

"I saw it in your file when I wondered why you kept putting everyone else's needs above your own," Dro said as Vikkas lifted his head and scanned the area for a moment. "Also confirmed it in the field when some of your habits made me question a few things."

"Because when I don't, people die."

Jax faced him and took in a breath that hurt entirely too much. Every effort they made to save Alia, it seemed that their enemies had already anticipated the moves. Almost feeling as caged in now as he had growing up. "You might have seen my file, but you don't know the biggest issues I had growing up. Hannah and Sofie never got enough to eat. Neither did the other kids in that place. I mean, no matter where they placed me, the threat was always the same. Do what you're told and don't ask for anything. Be grateful just to … breathe. And the ones who couldn't defend themselves got the worst of it."

Dro's face remained expressionless, but his eyes flashed with anger. Vikkas kept his focus on Jax, but his anger showed in the stiff set of his shoulders. Traffic slowed as onlookers tried to figure out if an accident caused the men to be on the side of the road holding what seemed to be an intense conversation.

There were good foster parents out there. Ones who love children, wanted them, and couldn't have them. Why couldn't the agency place them with people like that?

Alia gave him a long lingering look before maneuvering around Nasir to reclaim her seat in the car. He wanted to go to her, let her know that everything would be all right. But how could he lie to her when he had no idea how this would all turn out. Marrying her, a suggestion from Om Ali to have another name for her passport, had put her in greater danger.

"It was bad," Dro conceded. "I get it, man. But how does this equate to what we're facing now?"

"Because I understand the challenges we face on a deeper level. For girls, it's different," Jax answered. "From the moment they're born, for some of them there's never quite a safe place. Age doesn't matter." He ran his fingers through his hair. "I refused to tell the social worker about the broken arm my foster father gave me when I tried to put a stop to things. They would've pulled me out of that house, and no one would've been there to protect them. Someone had to be the buffer simply because we ended up with strangers after our parents checked out long before we could speak up for ourselves."

Vikkas and Dro moved in as Nasir leaned against the hood watching them intently. Alia peered from the window of the car, torn between remaining where she was and coming out to comfort Jax. The love she had for him was so amazing. When he told her that they would do an annulment once they made it to the states, she wouldn't hear of it. They were already friends, and they would find their way to love, and learn their way through life. Her words meant the world to him.

"You want to know why I didn't ask for help with this situation right away?" Jax asked.

Dro and Vikkas shared a glance before putting their focus back on him.

"Because half the time I was thrown into the fire and had to figure things out on my own. Having a team behind me does not always compute." He held up a hand to ward off the protest from Vikkas and Dro that was coming. "Yes, it's different with people connected to The Castle, but still, my first instinct is always ...."

Dro tried to place a hand on his arm, but Jax inched away.

"Where are they now?" Vikkas asked, sliding Dro a warning glance to let Jax have his space in this vulnerable moment.

Jax stared at the still waters for a moment. "Sophie was taken to a mental institution after they treated her for not just one, but an array of STDs, and she fell into a coma. Hannah didn't make it, either. She died in childbirth. She was only eleven. I couldn't always protect them like I wanted to; like they needed me to." Jax inhaled and let out a slow sigh. "If that can happen on American soil under the very watch of the institution that took us from parents to someplace that was supposed to be better, what do you think will happen if we leave Alia's sisters and cousins behind?"

He locked gazes with his wife across the distance, then continued with, "I know you all think it's about Alia, but all of the girls and women are in danger, and also Aunt Raja who was a widow, but still of child-bearing age. I would rather take Uncle Ibrahim's girls with us and ask forgiveness rather than permission. They're babies, just like ..." Jax closed his eyes getting his bearings for a moment. "Alia knows they aren't safe either. She won't leave without them. You can leave, but I'll stay here until they're out of here or Oded ends my life."

Jax struggled to force the sound of Fatima's laughter and Lotus's shy smile from his mind. They were both so different now than when he first arrived as though they knew something was wrong but couldn't put a voice to it. "When the Kings come up with the rest of an even better exit plan, take my wife, the little girls, Aunt Raja, and get them out. Don't worry about me."

Dro and Vikkas exchanged another wary glance before they swept Jax into a huddle.

"We'll do it your way," Dro agreed after a few moments. "We focus on the ones who are in the greatest amount of danger. I give you my word on that." Dro clasped Jax's shoulder. "But no way in hell are we leaving you here. You're our brother and we leave non behind."

CHAPTER 11

$\mathcal{T}$en Days before the Freedom Gala

"IT WILL BE EASY," Vikkas taunted, glaring at Dro while pacing in front of the fireplace with his Durabian passport in hand. "All we'll need is enough cash." He wrinkled his nose in disgust as he held his perspiration-soaked tunic away from his skin. "Noooooo, we don't need Durabian passports. We only need American ones."

Dro leaned against the stone wall separating the dining room from the kitchen and chuckled. "See, why do you want to bring up old stuff?"

That brought on a smile from Jax and Vikkas.

The walk from the hotel to Alia's home in the scorching heat had drained them. After the failed attempt yesterday, the two of them easily booked the two-bedroom suite, a spacious lodging that could house an entire family, which could literally be the case any day now that the tribunal was going after the rest of Nasir's property. They were the only two guests in the hotel since no one was traveling into the country.

After a visit with Om Ali's people, they found that their things had been ever so slightly disturbed. They didn't have the equipment to sweep for listening devices if they'd been planted. Meeting at Nasir's for these type of discussions wasn't the best option either because someone was always there, but it had served well so far. Sometimes they spoke in King Protocol as well as a limited form of Zaras language that most Ajidis failed to learn because it was "beneath" them. Other times sensitive information was written down and passed between them before being burned.

"Where's Alia," Vikkas asked, looking over Jax's shoulder.

"She's resting. They spent another day clearing out one of our properties ..." He ended there because the sorrowful expression on Aunt Raja's face sobered him. "Forgive me for being so bold, but I need to ask a question," Jax said slowly, measuring his words because he knew the next thing he said could be painful for Nasir to consider.

"I am almost afraid to say yes but go on." Nasir pulled four glasses and a bottle of sparkling pear juice from a nearby shelf.

Amal, a little boy who was in Aunt Raja's care, tipped in. His parents—both members of the police force—had been killed in the first of the invasion. The family wanted nothing to do with him since they had not approved of the mother's line of work. She had to keep her assignments hidden, but the moment the Balitan raided the Ministry of Defense, they procured the names of judges and all women in law enforcement and the military and turned them over to the men who had been freshly released from prison. The thirst for revenge was slaked with the blood of judges, police and Zaras who had put them behind bars. And since it was not the Balitan military who was committing these atrocious crimes, Oded claimed that he was investigating the "family dispute" that had "mysteriously" resulted in the deaths of so many women.

Jax immediately clamped down on what he was about to say,

waiting until the raven-haired boy with large brown eyes, much like Raja's, left the room. He seemed to be stalling over the choice of whatever pastry he wanted to have.

"Amal has a horrible sweet tooth," Raja said with a laugh. "Most times we indulge him."

He followed the path of Amal's movements, and the moment the little boy glanced over his shoulder, he locked gazes with Jax who settled more comfortably in the chair and rolled up his sleeves. Would his child also have a curious nature and a sweet tooth? Would he or she have Alia's smile and calm nature? Girl or boy? Simply healthy was enough for him. Simply alive was enough if they were able to navigate through these challenges.

His heart had actually hurt that morning when he carefully extracted himself from Alia's embrace. She moaned in her sleep, and it took everything in him to walk out to take that meeting with Dro, Vikkas and the men Om Ali designated as their resistance contacts, when all he wanted was to watch the sunrise before making love to her as the world began anew. Even with all this danger, she was his peace in the storm. She had loved him without even knowing who he truly was. She saw the best parts of him. Saw the heart of him. Wanted nothing more from him but his love and to allow her to be who she was meant to be.

Jax's mind flashed back to the day he first laid eyes on Alia. After completing his Middle East assignment in Qatar, Jax agreed to escort his mentor's fiancé's best friend back to the United States to attend their long-awaited wedding. He was told by Aunt Raja that he could find Alia in the market. Jax made his way to the open-air market where spices, grains, oils, and other goods were for purchase or trade. Jax identified Alia immediately. While making plans for her departure, Jax and Alia has spoken several times via video conference. He thought she was pretty and there was an instant attraction but the screen on his laptop or the multiple pictures of the two best friends, didn't do her justice. Alia was beautiful, and Jax's heart skipped several beats.

"Jax ... hello," Alia called out waving as she approached. "Welcome to Ajid."

He held her gaze, mesmerized by her lovely bright eyes. Her smooth skin was make-up free; her raven hair was covered by a purple silk scarf. She wore a simple teal ankle-length dress and open-toe sandals. While the outfit was appropriate wear for the environment, Jax couldn't help but wonder what she wore underneath it and how much he'd enjoy finding out. Jax wanted to kick his own butt for having such thoughts about Lola's best friend. A woman he figured was as innocent as she was beautiful.

He blinked a couple of times before saying, "Thank you."

"I apologize you had to track me down. I assume Aunt Raja told you I was here." Jax smiled and nodded, still unable to push past the lump in his throat. "I thought I'd be back before you arrived. I just wanted to pick up a few things for Lola. She loves the oils and spices you can only get on this side of the world."

"I know." He reached for the bags she held, and his hand grazed hers sending shockwaves throughout his body. Alia gasped, blushed, and quickly pulled her hand back. "Allow me."

"Th ...thank... you," she stuttered.

They stood staring into each other's eyes. There was an electrical pull between them that Jax recognized as desire. Something he knew Alia would hide if she could. She blinked, breaking the connection. "How was your trip?"

"It was fine. The jet is being serviced now so we'll be ready to leave tonight."

Alia talked as they made their way back to the house. She brought him up to speed on all the latest happenings as they traveled down the hot dirt road. Jax tried to focus on the words that crossed those lovely lips while keeping an eye out on their environment. Unfortunately, his heart and wayward body were responding to Alia in ways he's never experienced. Jax had a job to do and the last thing he expected was this type of complication.

As they approached the house, they saw police and several of Alia's family members that appeared to be waiting just for them, or for her. She was arrested for being part of a protest when the Balitan military took the capital and the first restrictions for women were handed down.

"Let's wait until he leaves before we say anything more," Jax said, pushing aside those wonderful thoughts of Alia and the angst that followed when the twelve officers held him back as another set of men escorted her to a vehicle. She signaled for Jax not to take action, but he didn't listen and ended up in handcuffs. "Ibrahim had a surprising amount of info that only was talked about in this room."

"You could not believe that Amal has been giving information to my brother about our discussions?" Nasir frowned and looked to Raja, whose face pulled into a mask of concern as she thought things over. "Surely my brother would not stoop so low as to use a child to—"

"I *know* he is," Jax countered as Raja closed her eyes, coming to the same realization. "Ibrahim mentioned a few things in conversation last night that were not said within your brother's hearing." Jax frowned at Nasir's shocked expression.

"You said you had a question for me?"

Vikkas tilted his head as he looked at Jax, waiting for him to query something the three of them had discussed last night.

"Are you sure your parents' accident did not come by your brother's hand?" Dro asked, when Jax didn't say anything.

The silence that followed the question was nothing short of alarming. Raja shuddered.

Nasir's hand trembled as he poured and set one glass in front of Jax then the others. "If you had asked me several weeks ago, I would have absolutely been offended. When Alia brought it up, I brushed it aside. Given the current state of things and his recent actions ..." Nasir shrugged. "I believe he may have had a hand in it to hurry the process along, believing it would work in his favor. He could not know what was in my father's Will or how the estate was formed. He knew he would inherit something. Now he realizes that it is not enough."

"No wonder he's in Oded's back pocket," Dro mused. "He wanted to find a legal way to discredit you and take over what's left of your family's fortune. They've frozen your assets and seized the properties."

"At the rate things are going, there won't be anything left to salvage," Jax said over the rim of his glass. "Even then, Ibrahim is going to have a battle with the revenue bureau when it comes to taxes because each bureau is running things different, and everyone has their hand out."

Nasir winced at that thought. "And this will totally do away with the Fadels in Ajid. Maybe that was the plan all along."

"I know it was," Vikkas said. "Oded's jealousy of you and your family runs deep."

"I always wondered ... I mean ... we planned everything right," Aunt Raja said. "We couldn't possibly foresee that Ibrahim would use a youngster to give our plan to the enemy."

Jax looked out the window in time to see Ibrahim as he ambled down the street, giving the royal wave to anyone he thought would stop and take a look at him in all his new finery. The timing of his visits was a little suspect.

"Ibrahim can't even look Nasir in the eye these days," Jax said, keeping his focus on the little boy who sidled up to Ibrahim to whisper something in his ear.

Today, Ibrahim wore a shemagh, the white cotton scarf worn about the head and held in place with a black cord known as an *agch*. The rings on his fingers were gaudy and suited him. Something about him reminded Jax of a slimy, used car salesman. Everything about him rang of double speak right down to his gimlet eyes that darted about the room. They matched his nervous jittering laugh that bordered on hysteria.

"He isn't even being slick about it," Dro said. "Every time you've paid Alia's fines and those new estate fees for the legal case, somehow, it's money that lands back into his pocket. I'm sure of it."

"Maybe what little conscience he has is kicking his ass." Dro nodded while observing Ibrahim had switched direction and was now on the path that led to the Tribunal Headquarters and palaces.

"Greed is driving his moral compass and we're paying the price," Jax said, dropping down in a chair across from Vikkas, but watching Nasir and Raja take notice of Ibrahim talking to Amal. "Thankfully, he hasn't been let in on the bigger issues we're figuring out."

"Do tell?" Vikkas said, as his shoulders swayed in time with the sounds of Radhika's lyrical chant floating from the speakers in Aunt Raja's room. "From what I understand, this house in the wealthier area of the village is the last piece of property the family owns. Everything else was caught up in an illegal land grab by elite members of the tribunal who have been part of the estate lawsuit brought by Ibrahim."

"Our brother has yet to understand that there would be nothing left when they are done," Raja said.

Jax took in a slow breath as dread settled in once more.

"That's not the issue we're talking about," Dro said. "For starters, we're assuming that her uncle doesn't know that newly-weds are on deck."

Vikkas walked past the chaise, took a sip from a bottle of water before tossing the other to Dro. "How do you know for sure he isn't aware of the marriage?"

Dro caught the bottle midair and placed it next to his half-filled glass. "Because he wouldn't keep pitting Oded against Nasir this way. Oded would feel deceived and dear old 'Unc's' meal ticket and assurance that he would win the estate suit would be out the window."

"And that is if they do not bury him in a hole with a bag filled with scorpions first," Raja said. "Oded has always taken betrayal and incompetence personally."

Vikkas took another swig and placed his bottle on the table next to a tray of baklava, figs, and grapes that Aunt Raja always had ready for them just ahead of an amazing entree. "With the fact that he has publicly told the world he's marrying Alia, they can nullify a marriage to an American. They can't make the biological results of a child go away."

"They can," Nasir said in a dry tone. "We will not like their methods."

Jax snagged the bottle from the table and after a few swallows of the lukewarm water, he waited as the liquid settled hard on his stomach. "Once they find out her true status, Oded will not want to marry her. But because she's tied to so much American money, he'll still want her as something else that would keep me up at night."

Vikkas let out a low whistle. "None of that will come into play. They cannot override a Durabian passport or hold one of its citizens."

"At this point, I wouldn't put anything past them," Jax said.

CHAPTER 12

*N*ine Days Before the Freedom Gala

"ALL OF THIS CONTROL. What are they protecting us from? The only ones who commit crimes ... are men." She said as she continued kneading the dough for preparations of tonight's dinner. "Auntie, I am so sorry for causing all of this trouble,"

"Do not worry yourself," Raja replied. "This was bound to happen. It's all about men who cannot handle rejection. Men who feel entitled. Oded has always been the man to control everything and everyone. He cannot take the fact that you, of all people, do not want him. He always gets what he wants. Unfortunately, because of your exotic beauty and bounty, you are like the grand prize in some contest."

Raja moved soundlessly toward the oven to check the heat. "So many men here don't understand that the world is changing, and they are losing so much by leaving women out of the equation.

Our world would be so much more advanced if they respected who we are and what we contribute."

"Now our family is paying the price and there is nothing I can do."

Raja placed her flour covered hands gently over Alia's. "Live your life, Alia. Love that young man. He's going to make sure you and the little one have a better life in America than you ever could have here."

"I know, but what of you, Fatima, and Lotus? They're flowers." She whispered. "They'll never leave you alone when we leave. They are years away from having monthlies, but they will be wives before this is all said and done."

"Not if we figure out how to get around the way they are trying to shut down the last of our businesses, the restaurant, the laundry, and the textiles. All those beautiful fabrics. At least we've been able to get most of the clothes out and to those families in need."

Simi slithered into the room with discontent written all over her face. Instead of waiting to be invited into the conversation she barged right in. "The older women in the villages rely on their needlework to buy food, yarn and whatever else they need to support themselves. So many people are losing their jobs and new ones are not opening. People are being thrust into sudden poverty, including us. It doesn't seem worth it. How bad can this marriage to Oded be?"

"So bad that your father will never allow it to happen," Raja said. "Men talk and the things that he's heard..." She shuddered at the thought. "He would die before he let Oded get his hands on either one of you. Maybe we should do something ourselves rather than sitting around talking."

"Everything is well in hand," Alia said to her aunt and sister. "We shouldn't interfere."

Simi gave them a sly smile over her shoulder as she left the room.

When the coast was clear, Aunt Raja said, "We might have to do exactly that, because you're going to show soon. Then there will be problems we cannot fix." Aunt Raja paced the bedroom Alia and Jax secretly shared at night. "Your new man is moving too slow. Twins run in our family and if you are carrying two, you will flush out sooner than they realize."

Alia gasped and gripped her head with both hands. "Twins? I can barely wrap my mind around having one child. I surely want Father to come with us." She reached for her aunt's hands. "You must come with us, too. I want all of us to be there. I won't feel happy knowing you're still in danger."

Raja settled on the bed next to Alia and placed a hand on her abdomen. "You all have a full life ahead of you. Unfortunately, ours is winding down," she said with a wan smile. "Here is all we know. There was beauty here once. In time, it will come again. The problems we face will not be solved before you escape. Let us focus on you right now."

"I miss mother so much." Alia sobbed. resting her head on her aunt's shoulder.

"That could not be helped, either." She said smoothing a hand over Alia's hair. "Siobhan was not safe here. The treatment was getting worse, and your father would have been forced to give his life to save hers." Raja stilled her movements. "The fact that Oded's father had hinted at sharing her even in jest showed his state of mind. Soon, by the response others were thinking the same thing. That she was an American and had low values and should be offered to men who desired her. So, we feared that she would disappear, and we would all know who had taken her, but nothing could be done."

A moment went by, and the sudden silence made Raja tip to the door and shut it completely. "You should have seen how angry Oded was when he came unexpectedly for dinner, and Siobhan was not here. He demanded to know where she had gone. The answer did not sit well with him. No one expected her to leave Ajid without Nasir. They had a watch on him, never realizing that he would do what was best for his wife. That is when they put a tighter rein on who could travel and when. That is what is making things so hard to get you away from here. They knew you would be next, and to be honest, they were right. They realized Jax came here for a reason."

"It's unfortunate that the police do not get involved in local disputes. Especially when it involves marriages, and one is with a power player. If the daughters left with Siobhan, it would have sent up red flags. A single person on a journey, not so much."

"They have their own corruption going." Aunt Raja shook her head slowly. "Never saw a place take such a turn so fast. This is the wrong place to be a woman."

"This is the right place, wrong time." Alia slid a glance to Aunt Raja. "We were making so much progress, so many strides in women's rights. Now they want to put women back to a time where we couldn't leave the house without a male, let alone hold down a job."

Raja stroked a thumb across Alia's cheek.

"Do you think they would put father in prison if we managed to escape?"

"There is that possibility, but he can take what they will do," Raja answered, giving Alia's hand a gentle pat. "You could not take being in the prison of marriage to Oded."

"Do you truly believe that Uncle Ibrahim would betray us for money?"

Raja scoffed with a flourish of her hand. "He would betray his own mother for money, if she was still alive."

"Yes, by all means we have to watch out for him." Alia said, "We keep the circle small, and it is less likely that the information will fall into the wrong ears. I am regretting that Simi and Kamala know so much. At least, I know that Simi is only sneaking out to be with friends. Kamala is on something else entirely."

Aunt Raja sighed and stroked a hand in Alia's hair. "Jaxon suits you. It is wise that he waits until the house falls silent to come to you. The daylight hours must feel like an eternity."

"They are. Keeping up appearances is killing me," Alia admitted. "Never thought I would live to see the day that I resented the daylight, but I do. Sometimes, it's like I'm not even married."

"Patience, my dear. Waiting will make everything even sweeter." Aunt Raja smiled. "You will have the rest of your lives to enjoy each other."

"If we make it out of here in one piece," Alia added.

Raja sighed, and there was a world of weariness in that one sound. "You used to be such an optimist, Alia."

"I live in a place where women's rights are being taken away," she protested. "I live in a place where it wasn't safe for my mother to live. I live in a place where it's not safe for me or any woman. I cannot be optimistic about anything anymore."

"That life growing within you is proof that the world should go on." Raja placed a hand on Alia's belly. "Proof that we all should keep living and have an opportunity to change things."

"You all did that thirty years ago and what happened?" She shot back, moving away. "All of your handiwork is slowly being reversed. They're just waiting for the last day Americans are to be totally out of the area. Now they will be pouncing like a lion on prey."

Raja smiled, and it was more frightening than her anger had been. "But even the lion gets eaten one day."

CHAPTER 13

$\mathcal{E}$ight Days Before the Freedom Gala

JAXON IS MY RIB.

That quiet, yet profound knowledge settled Alia's spirit like morning dew on the petals of a thirsty flower. She traced his smile with a finger, wondering if the warm pressure of his lips against hers had left a mark that someone could see. Thankfully the love marks Jax left all over her body, especially in the most intimate of places, would never be seen by anyone other than her husband. She was careful about being around one another where prying eyes would discern the truth, but Jax had the hardest time. And that touched her in no small way.

The deep lines of concern on his face made it clear that the failed trip to the airport had taken its toll.

Later that night when they were turned away at the airport checkpoint, Jaxon had opened up to her about his past. Learning more of Jax's background had been disheartening but explained so much about him. He had finally found a home with her family and had, somehow in the process, become their knight in shining armor. So had the other men he had brought in. Lola had said the Kings were amazing, and she was right. Dro was going to be the perfect husband for her friend. Vikkas, with his interesting sense of humor, had such a keen grasp on the situation. They could have left when they had the opportunity, but stayed and made the Fadel family problems their own. They were honorable men, like her father.

Many had benefited from Nasir's efforts in the community, but it was hard to know who to trust. When the rumors spread that Oded had formed his own military, a network of men who were not afraid to assist came together—Om Ali, Nasir, and a few others. All others had caved so quickly, it was as though there had been some secret signal given to everyone that this was going to happen and if they fought, they would die. Amal's parents had stood up with the forces that tried to fight. They paid the ultimate price.

They told her The Castle men were some of the most powerful ones on the planet. If they were anything like Jax, Dro and Vikkas, she believed it. And she had hope that her family would be safe—all of them.

At the moment, Jax, Dro, Nasir, and Vikkas were delivering food to widows and orphans. In addition, they helped to build several miniature windmills to convert wind power into rotational energy so the people in those areas did not rely on a grid and could provide heat, light and a way to prepare meals. The Castle also had solar panels smuggled in and the men showed women and men alike how to affix them to houses as another energy source.

They also passed out seeds to grow gardens and soybeans to feed themselves since the food sources were becoming scarce. They helped implement a system where they could take care of each other, and any of the few men who remained would take on the responsibility of escorting the women if they needed to be out and about. Each day, they used those opportunities and the locations to secretly connect with members of Om Ali's resistance to get intel and pass on instructions.

Simi sulked in one corner of the kitchen, thumbing through her cell phone while Alia prepared a tray of fruit for Jax and his Castle brothers who were set to arrive soon.

"Your efforts are wasted on those Americans, sister," Simi taunted with a dismissive wave of her freshly manicured hand. Which was a little surprising since all of the salons were closed and so were any stores that sold beauty products to women. "Why won't you listen to Uncle Ibrahim and marry Oded?"

Kamala nodded, looking to Alia for an answer that would not come. Rather than respond, Alia retrieved a bottled water from the basket beside her sister and returned to reclaim a seat at the tabletop island situated in the center of the kitchen.

Alia smiled as Fatima and Lotus ran through on their way to the sunroom—the special place she had created for them to learn English and some of the American customs. She called for them to come back, then handed both children a pita filled with falafel, tomatoes, and tahini sauce before playfully shooing them away as Jax's deep baritone voice drifted to her on the early evening air.

As she picked up some refreshments and entered the family room to greet him, her steps slowed to a halt as revulsion washed over her. Uncle Ibrahim stood admiring himself in the mirror above the hearth.

Her heart went south at the sight of the round barrel of an old man as he extended those sausage-like fingers to show off the gemstones and platinum settings on several rings glittering under the lights.

"Uncle Ibrahim, those are some mighty fine garments you're sporting," Alia said as she locked gazes with Jax who shifted his focus from the notes he'd organized on maps and schematics that Om Ali's son had secured. He quickly scooped them up and tucked them under some more innocent-looking paperwork.

Ibrahim nearly jumped out of his skin, but immediately recovered and straightened his shoulders. "Oh, this old thing? Purchased it on sale."

Jax gave her uncle a lengthy onceover. "Looks custom-made to me," he quipped, taking the tray from Alia's hands before offering her a chair near the open window, making sure some distance remained between the two of them. Ibrahim had been very vocal about demanding that she marry into the Farhat family from the day she arrived. She had been equally as vocal that it would never happen. "What is that? Your third outfit today?"

Ibrahim glared at Jax for a long while, those beady eyes shifting as he tried to come up with a plausible answer. No one else dressed so regally every single day, three changes of clothes per day. "Well, the material is not as expensive as I would like. The labor is merely passable." He plucked an imaginary piece of lint from his robes and gave himself one last appraising look before turning to face them.

"You never wore so much jewelry before," Alia hedged, flickering a look to Jax, who gave her an almost imperceptible nod that her observations, and voicing them were spot on. Ibrahim's cheeks had flushed with a reddish color.

A dark shadow passed over Ibrahim's face before his lips split in a nervous smile. "A man cannot have nice things without people being suspicious, my precious niece?"

"Sure, if it's not out of character for that man," she countered with an equally pleasant smile. "Thanks to your ... friends, this family is struggling with simple things." She also did a lengthy perusal from the top of his head to his expensive shoes. "Yet, you're sporting two years' worth of groceries on your right hand. And you don't have any kind of job or money to speak of since it's all tied up in the estate lawsuit that hasn't had any real movement in months."

Jax beckoned for Alia to come closer to his side, but she held her ground. Ibrahim lifted his head in a haughty manner that was all too familiar these days. As though he was above it all—the struggles, the anxiety, and the fear hanging over them.

"I have investments. Besides, these are heirlooms, belonged to our parents." He paused and held his hand up. "I would rather cut off my fingers than see our history sold like Persian rugs in the open market."

"Investments where? The brothels in town?" Alia shot back, trying to ignore Jax's warning glance. She was tired of holding her tongue when it was so obvious her uncle had betrayed them in the worst way. Every family had a Judas, and Judas had loved Christ, but still betrayed him all the same. Ibrahim had always been jealous of Nasir, so he definitely had the kind of heart that would take thirty pieces of silver.

"I just find it strange that you suddenly have all of this money stashed away somewhere, but you cry poor when it comes time to chip in for the family to help us when the tribunal keeps levying all these fines."

"You are the reasons for those. Why should I pay for your mistakes?" His beady eyes flashed, and face darkened with an ugliness that left no doubt of his rage. "That university education gave you the tongue of a serpent, I see. Well, if you must know, I have people who matter," he said in a lower tone. "Sponsors."

"Oded and his family," she accused. "Tribunal members who are promising to give you a seat with the leaders, but it means serving up your family first."

Ibrahim waddled across the room, aiming in her direction. "And you need to mind your manners and watch the way you speak to me."

Jax's strides ate up the ground until he blocked Ibrahim's path. "How about I mind it for her?" he asked, making sure that Ibrahim, who had been quick to strike Lotus and Fatima, did not take out his displeasure on Alia. He had been warned more than once that it would not be a pretty outcome. Jax had finally curtailed the man's mistreatment of his daughters—but that mean streak still reared its head from time to time.

The older man gave him a disdainful glare before backing away. "You American interlopers need to stay out of our family business."

"And how is Oded and his father?" Jax shot back, ignoring the fists balled at Ibrahim's side. "You've been speaking with them quite often lately. Surprising, given what they're doing to this family. And it's also strange that they haven't given you what they promised."

She glanced over to Nasir, who entered the room carrying the rest of the meal and several bowls of water to wash their hands. A not subtle reminder that Dro and Vikkas would arrive soon. Hopefully, Ibrahim would be gone before then. Normally they timed things just right with someone giving them a heads up on tribunal meetings—impromptu and otherwise, but Ibrahim was lingering for another reason.

"So those other Americans are on the way?" Ibrahim said with a sly smile taking in the set up. "Maybe I will stay for dinner after all."

Alia gripped the armrest and pulled herself to her feet. "Excuse me, Father, but all of a sudden, I'm very tired. I can come back down in a while and help you clean up after he's gone."

The day had been hard enough and the last thing she wanted to deal with was Ibrahim. Alia, Aunt Raja, Lotus, and Fatima had spent the day in the last of their family restaurants selling off equipment and giving away their remaining supplies and spices to those families and widows who were even less fortunate than them. Alia was overwhelmed standing in the empty space which was once filled with joy, laughter and families enjoying meals courtesy of recipes that had been in their family for years. Large square tables with couch style seating were filled with platters of delicious smelling and tasting food.

Alia closed her eyes remembering how the room was once

decorated in bright rich colors, cream-painted walls decorated with deep red, gold, and purple-colored tapestries and colorful drapes decorated the ceilings. There were rare relics and artifacts on full display throughout the restaurant. These were the memories she'd always hold dear and share with their family. Memories she'd take with her if they made it out of Ajid alive.

CHAPTER 14

"*N*o need to help with cleaning," Jax said, eyeing Aunt Raja who slipped out to give Dro and Vikkas a heads up that Ibrahim was still home. "I'll take care of this. You get some rest." He raised an eyebrow and gave her a slight nod as if to say, *'We got this.'* She glanced at her uncle one last time and gave Jax a curt nod of her own before sweeping out of the room.

"I want you to leave," Nasir said gritting his teeth. "You have upset my daughter and that will not do."

"Women are far too emotional. Men are born to be reasonable. You are making too much of things. Oded and his father are misunderstood," Ibrahim said with a little laugh and a dismissive shrug as Raja came . "They are only trying to solidify the long-time union between our families—Ajidi and Zaras. That is all. You are the head of this household and are being stubborn. That is where the problem lies."

He glanced in the direction Alia had gone. "She is nothing special. She held a position at the medical center, taking the place of a far more deserving man. And she is not even full blood. And taking up the cause of Zaras when she should have stayed invisible. She should be elated that any man in Ajid wants her now." He clasped his hands tightly with a broad smile splitting his face. "Especially one so high up in the regime that has finally taken his rightful place. You should have served her up to Oded a long time ago." He pointed to his wedding ring. "But without fail, she will be well taken care of in proper fashion and learn the culture she was born into before you ran off to hide in America like a coward."

Jax signaled to Aunt Raja to slide out and alert Dro and Vikkas to tip upstairs until Ibrahim left.

"I did not run! What opportunities were there for my wife and daughters? You have such disdain for America, yet you want to benefit from what I gained." Nasir shook his head. "Oded only wants her because of her mixed heritage. As husband, he wouldn't be duty bound to treat her with even a modicum of respect he would give a full blood. He will treat her as he has done all the women he considers beneath him and I will be unable to protect her." Nasir set the last tray of kebabs down with such a clatter that caused the contents to nearly fall to the floor.

"You could not possibly know that," Ibrahim said with a heavy sigh, while moving until they stood nearly toe to toe.

"Brother, people talk. He boasts about what he does to them and has no fear of any consequence. And that was *before* he rose to this level of power. I know his exact plans for my daughter and none of them are good." Nasir lifted a towel that was slung across his shoulder and spread it over the tray before maneuvering past his brother until he stood next to Jax. "My daughter deserves better."

The message was crystal.

"She will be well cared for," Ibrahim roared, shaking a fist at Nasir. "More than she is here. Barely enough food to feed yourself, let alone, this family."

"And the reason we are struggling is because you have helped them cut off all revenue streams," Nasir yelled back ignoring Jax's steady grip on his arm. "Trying to force my hands by having inspectors close down our businesses for personal reasons is dishonest. Our father built his enterprise from nothing. He cultivated connections without the help of anyone else."

"Then he trusted you with the estate when you lived halfway around the globe," Ibrahim countered, his tone was as bitter as his expression. "Where are those powerful American connections when you need them? Put away your pride and accept their offer, Nasir," Ibrahim warned as he went back to his reflection to admire the sweep of his robe while buffing one of the stones jutting from the rings on his left hand.

"Oded and his father can help you in so many ways." He leveled a steely gaze at his brother. "They can harm you as well." Ibrahim spread his hands out, a gesture resembling a plea of some sort. "Think of the opportunities for us, brother. You will be a respected man here in Ajid again and also have a seat among the ruling class. Something rare for Zaras. We will finally have a voice in how this country is run."

"Uncle is right. You are losing favor in this community," Simi added, sliding into the room, and popping a grape in her red mouth. "There are now bets being waged on whether we will ever recover without marrying into the Farhat family. Kamala said we must, or we will die."

Nasir gave Jax's shoulder a squeeze to keep him silent. "Ibrahim, if they cannot find monetary satisfaction by marrying my daughters, who are of age, who do you think they will come for next?"

Ibrahim's smile faded as he faced them once more. "Never mind about my Fatima and Lotus. They are pure bloods and bound to marry well and bear many children. You should want your daughters to have the same," he said, but there was a hiccup in his voice that signaled concern. As well he should. He might ignore things when it came to his nieces, but was his heart really so hard that he did not care an ounce for his own daughters?

"No," Nasir disagreed. "My daughters are not chattel. They

85

deserve to be married to men of *their* choosing. You on the other hand, want mine to marry men just like you."

Ibrahim's face flushed a tinge of red. "The problem is you believe your girls are special. Believe they are better with all that American education. Spoiled is what they are. And they are trying to taint my girls with such nonsense as fairness and equality."

Nasir eased past Jax to stand directly in front of his brother. Ibrahim outweighed him by a good one hundred pounds and towered over him by at least five inches, but thanks to the personal self-defense techniques Jax had shown him, Alia's father could handle his business without any assistance from Jax. "Women have never been important to you. That is why your wife left you so suddenly. Even she could only take so much."

Raja tucked her head in and gestured upward with an index finger.

Jax sucked in a breath as Ibrahim looked down on Nasir as though he were something he'd stepped on by accident. "And when I find her—"

"You will *never* lay eyes on Indira again," Nasir replied with a certainty that put a chill in the room. "My only issue is that she didn't take her daughters. She had the mistaken belief that you knew their value and would see that no harm would come to them. How wrong she was. You never laid a hand on them before but have no problem doing so now."

"She will need a divorce at some point." Ibrahim smirked and plopped down in a seat at the head of the table.

Jax glanced at his watch, trying to get Nasir to cut off this line of conversation that was getting his brother riled up again. They had to get Ibrahim out of the house. Dro and Vikkas were supposed to partake of a meal, share the latest intel, then slide out to meet with one of Om Ali's connections who was helping with transport and another who was getting them the rest of the schematics to the outposts, roads leading to the airport as well as the trade port buildings. Om Ali was also trying to secure transport for the women who were in hiding, shifting them from safehouse to safehouse, all while showing a public face at the tribunal headquarters each day. A dangerous game he was playing, but his heart had always been on the side of human rights for everyone.

"Seems like she's happy enough where she is without the official cutting of ties," Nasir said with a smile that Jax knew would infuriate Ibrahim and cause them to come to blows. "You have to take ownership for what happened in your marriage. When a wife is happy, there is no need for her to escape under the cover of darkness."

"Escape?" Ibrahim screeched, eyes widening to the size of plates. "Escape what? I gave Indira everything a woman could want."

Nasir wagged a finger as though he was speaking to a toddler. "No brother. You gave her everything *you* wanted her to have. Two different things. And evidently the life you provided was not enough. She felt it would never be enough or that you would kill her at the rate you were carrying on. How many times did she have to seek medical treatment?"

Ibrahim made a wide berth around Nasir to grab a few grapes. He popped one into his mouth, then rattled the rest like dice. "Women should only want what we give them. We provide for them, not the other way around. If you have not schooled your daughters as such, they are in for a hard life here in Ajid."

He tried to pick through the remainder of the food with his sweaty bare hands.

Jax wrinkled his nose in disgust and made a mental note to toss the top layer on both the fruit and bread trays before anyone else could consume them.

"Tell me, brother," Nasir taunted, causing Jax to brace himself for the next verbal blow to come. "Why are you so upset about Indira? After all, you do not have to provide for her now."

"No one embarrasses me that way." His glare intensified as his fist shook dangerously close to Nasir's face. "And I know your wife had something to do with it. Indira disappeared not long after Siobhan scurried off to America; like the Zaras rat she is."

Nasir did not move, showing how unfazed he was by his brother's tirade. Then he took the chair closest to the hearth and studied Ibrahim for a moment. "My wife went for an entirely different reason." He ran a thumb over the simple band of gold on his left hand and took in a breath that seemed to absorb every other sound in the room. "We all know she was not safe here. I loved her enough to let her go. You only love yourself—oh, and money. You need to take responsibility for what failed in your marriage, which is the main source of your anger and resentment. Just because you can treat a woman in a beastly manner does not mean you should."

Jax inwardly cringed at that hard truth. And no amount of telling a man like his brother would bear fruit. So why was he poking the bear?

Ibrahim gave him a toothy grin as he crammed a few more grapes into his mouth. "You have a lot of words for a man who does not have his wife."

"Siobhan didn't leave because she hates me," Nasir shot back, his voice holding a conviction that made Ibrahim stiffen. "She left because I love her."

"And what of him?" Ibrahim questioned, gesturing in Jax's direction. "Alia has been spending too much time with that American and his friends. The appearance of being alone without proper chaperones can get her stoned." He gave Jax a disdainful onceover. "Do you know that is also grounds to have her purity tested? Alia must be intact to become Oded's wife, or you will suffer far worse, and she, as well. You are not under American laws any longer. You are in Ajid now and it is rightfully under Balitan rule."

"And you are holding this falsehood of the Americans being a danger to Alia because ...?" Jax asked, his focus solely on the robust man

Ibrahim opened his wide mouth, then shut it quickly. A few moments later he said, "I just know, that is all."

Nasir's shoulders slumped with defeat. His brother's greed and quest for power knew no bounds or reason.

"More likely, you made promises to them you won't be able to keep," Jax said, taking the seat beside his father-in-law.

"We will see," Ibrahim replied in a sing song tone, but his eyes betrayed the malice within. "You are not the only one gifted in business or playing the long game, brother of mine. I know you think the Americans will help you. I have it on good authority that soon, they will not be able to help themselves."

With that, he swept from the house, a spring in his step as though what he had done to his family was no small thing.

CHAPTER 15

*S*even Days Before the Freedom Gala

"THEY HAVE GIVEN us the last round of business citations." Nasir handed the documents to Jax before settling down at the table. "This is for the ones where Raja held a silent seventy percent stake. They could not have known that unless Ibrahim had served them up. We have also lost the last of our real estate holdings entirely. They already made a land grab for the remaining pieces of my father's properties—those that are tied into the estate suit, which means even when the case will finally be heard there will be nothing left to fight for." His expression collapsed into one of despair as Jax examined the papers. "The tribunal's laws are so tainted. They want to put a chokehold on all the people who did not side with Oded."

Jax poured his father-in-law a mug of tisane, a hot herbal tea made from fruit, seeds, and spices. Alia was in the sunroom with Lotus and Fatima, teaching them more about American customs and language because she—ever the optimist—believed at some point, they would need it.

Nasir accepted it in both hands and took a sip. His red-rimmed eyes drifted over the surface of the table before returning to Jax's face. He was putting up an amazing show of strength—tears he dared not spill in front of his family.

"That is their plan. For us to sink so low financially, that we have no choice but to turn to them. That will never happen."

"I think we need to stop saying that word *never*," Raja warned, plaiting her hair into her signature braid. "Every time you do, it is put to the test."

There was a frightening amount of truth in that statement.

After skimming through the latest documents that arrived by tribunal messenger at the crack of dawn, it took everything in Jax not to rip the papers in half and toss them into the fire. Instead, he folded them before pushing them back across the table as Aunt Raja walked over to the stove to stir a rich chicken and vegetable stew.

"What about Uriel? Can you not ask him for help, brother?" She tapped the spoon on the pot, replaced the lid and busied herself with arranging freshly baked bread on a blue earthenware plate.

"I already asked," Nasir said and shook his head. "My old schoolmate directed me to do as Oded desired. He also told me that the tribunal was close to giving Ibrahim that seat they promised. Then he had the gall to tell me that he put in his own request to have Lotus the very moment she flowers."

"You mean, when she is of legal age?" Jax winced, knowing "flowers"—a menstrual cycle—happened between ages ten and twelve, far too young for marriage and the expectations that came with it.

"Legal and traditional are two different things here," Raja whispered as she flinched at some private pain, then returned to stirring their meal.

Jax put his attention on Nasir, who was still nursing the tisane, and waited for the man to face him.

"He has many other options for his son," Jax said, flickering a worried gaze between Nasir and Raja. "Why would he want a girl barely out of single digits for a daughter-in-law?"

Nasir's weary sigh made Jax's stomach fall to his toes. The angry tears that threatened to spill from Nasir's eyes were nothing compared to the pain that made him look even more ancient. Jax truly believed that the weight of that decision to return to his homeland to tie up his father's estate was plaguing him. He could not have known that Ibrahim had purposely done things so everything would eventually be ruled in Ibrahim's favor and that the man had promised his daughters in marriage to a tyrant.

"Uriel wasn't asking for his son," Nasir said before he retrieved a handkerchief from his pocket and swiped at his eyes. "He was asking for himself."

That admission brought everyone to a standstill. Aunt Raja released a whelp that brought a stab of angst to Jax's heart.

"So, it goes without saying that Dro was right," Vikkas mused. "All the girls in your family need to make that exit stage left, along with Aunt Raja, who is a widower, but can still carry someone's heir."

"I mean, if it is not too much trouble," Nasir said, pushing his beverage away.

"I'll reach out to our contact and get more Durabian passports," Vikkas said, preparing to leave. "They keep reminding me that when the numbers keep increasing, so does the danger level."

"I am willing to stay and face Oded and his father," Nasir said. "They may punish me, but—"

"I'm not leaving *anyone* behind," Jax said, cutting through any suggestion that they would abandon him to such a deadly fate. Alia would never have a moment's sleep if her father was not safe. "Not you, and not Aunt Raja, not anyone."

"You may not have a choice," Nasir said, locking gazes with Jax. "We men can fend for ourselves."

"The tribunal will not be kind when they bring you up on charges of treason," Raja warned, placing her back against the door to keep an eye out for anyone trying to listen in. "And they will consider it so because of those who disappear. Especially Ibrahim's daughters who he's already promised to other families so he can wash his hands of them."

Nasir gave Jax a smile that didn't quite reach his eyes. "It won't matter as long as my daughters, my dear sister, and nieces are safe and out of reach."

"And as far as that is concerned," Aunt Raja added, "Oded cannot lay any legal claim because there isn't a written covenant concerning marriage between Alia and Oded, or the other girls. That can only come from their father if he is still alive. And that is important in this part of the world. Nasir might have recourse, but if they follow through with any plans to force Alia into the marriage, the damage would be done by then. Taking up the issue with a higher court—an Islamic Emirate tribunal from surrounding countries that share the same religious belief, will be met with a lukewarm effort at righting that kind of wrong."

Jax held up a set of silver envelopes that were delivered by a tribunal courier. "Oded plans to publicly marry them at his freedom celebration. That coincides with the last day of the treaty where Americans have to be out of the country. Doing so legitimizes them to the world. They will not give Alia, Simi and Kamala or Nasir a chance to deny. Especially with Ibrahim speaking for them."

Jax glanced at Amal who was pilfering sugar cubes from a jar in the cupboard. Nasir turned and scowled at him. The boy cringed, nearly bumping into Aunt Raja on the way out. "Ouch."

Raja saw the look that Jax gave Amal and sent him outside to the garden.

"Why this sudden concern with Amal?" Nasir asked, placing a

hand on Jax's arm, summoning his attention back to their conversation.

"Not so sudden. I already mentioned that Amal has been spending too much time with Ibrahim these days. He also doesn't seem to be as hungry as everyone else. Barely eats at any meal that is served." Jax looked off in the direction Amal had gone and saw the moment the little boy turned and peered at them briefly before ducking behind a wall, hoping he wouldn't be seen. "Amal, go outside like your aunt said," Jax told him. "Go into the garden where we can see you."

He nodded and they waited until a scurry of footsteps sounded, then faded.

"Give a child who is missing his father a little more attention, and you can get whatever you want from them," Jax said, saddened that he had been so focused on the girls, that he had spent only a little time with Amal.

"You sound as if you speak from experience," Nasir said.

Jax gave a half shrug before responding, "Not for me. Not really hard to miss a man who chose everything and everyone over you." Jax waved off the sad look in the old man's eyes because the focus should not be on his past when their future was in jeopardy. "Ancient history. Now about Amal—"

Nasir leaned forward and gripped his arm. Despite the uncomfortable show of strength, Jax didn't pull back. "Permit me to be selfish, Jaxon Malone. You are a good man and will be an even greater husband. Your father's loss is my great gain, yes?" He released Jax after a nod and a smile of understanding, then grabbed the tisane and took a healthy sip.

Jax tried to swallow at the memories filling his mind which rendered him unable to speak. The kindness of the man before him was nearly his undoing. Not only had Nasir, a world away from Jaxon's harsh childhood, chosen him to keep his daughter safe, but also to help as many family members as possible. No, this exodus wouldn't end with this old man being beaten and bloody in the square like so many women and other protestors. He had pledged a personal oath to get the entire family out even if it meant staying behind.

"As for Amal, I will speak with him," Nasir offered while Raja placed the plate of bread, a small bowl of honey, and a saucer of oils and spices in the center of the table.

"No, leave it be. We don't want Ibrahim to know we're on to him," Jax warned. "But we could use Amal to feed misinformation." He tore a piece of bread and dipped it in the sweet amber substance.

"I do not want a child used that way," Nasir protested, but Raja pursed her lips to keep in her thoughts. She also seemed to share the same concern.

"He is already being used," Raja said as Jax placed the next bit of bread into his mouth. "Now I want to know what Ibrahim has promised our little friend for bringing our information to him."

Nasir grabbed a piece of bread and mirrored Jax's action but chose the savory oil and spices instead of the honey.

Jax pushed the bowl closer to Nasir while the honey, with a hint of clove, coated his tongue. "It's obviously food or treats of some type. Amal doesn't realize how odd it looks when he doesn't partake."

"Neither does Ibrahim," Nasir mused, with the tisane halfway to his mouth to wash down the last bite. "I understand your reasoning, but I still do not have to like it. Children are made to do all sorts of horrible things because the adults around them have no honor."

Jax absorbed that for a moment. "Well, you're not wrong about that. One of the foster families I lived with made the children in their care physically fight over what little food they gave us. The adults watched the whole thing and took bets from friends who came to watch. Whatever I won, I gave to the youngest ones," Jax said, remembering how grateful they were and how upset the bullies in the household were. "They loved to take on easy prey. And they certainly consider us prey by cornering us this way."

Jax tried to ignore the sorrowful look in Nasir's eyes. Receiving this type of warmth from people outside of his Castle family was new to him. "It's all right. I survived and Oded is wrong." He sat up straighter, getting his bearings and shaking off the bitter feelings that always accompanied those childhood memories. "This is different and does not harm Amal to make sure he has the wrong information to keep Ibrahim off the scent."

Nasir grimaced, then nodded. So did Raja.

"Dro and Vikkas want to get my observations on the layout of the trading ports to make proper plans. Also, I have to place a call to Daron and Calvin."

"Are those the other men with that Castle place you mentioned? You said there were many others—Kings, Queens, Knights ... so why are those two men the only ones you are contacting for such a big task?" Nasir asked, settling back in the chair once more to cradle the mug in both hands. Raja refreshed the cup but paused as Alia rushed through the kitchen, supporting Lotus as she sobbed into her shoulder and Fatima seemed to be walking in a trance.

Both men stood as Raja stacked both hands on her hips, watching them closely.

"Don't mind us, Auntie. Ibrahim explained what is going to happen to them after the Freedom Celebration. He said that as a woman and their caretaker, you should have discussed it with her already. He was pretty brutal and graphic about telling them what they are expected to do. Almost as if he enjoyed inflicting this pain upon them," Alia said, answering the unspoken question before the trio disappeared upstairs.

Jax stared after them before catching Nasir studying him. He bowed his head as if to answer some silent query of his own.

"If this is how things will go, Ibrahim will send Lotus and

Fatima to Oded the night of the celebration," Aunt Raja said. "None of the girls—yours or his—will be coming home."

"If Ibrahim has already signed a marriage contract for them," Alia said. "Then it's going to be very risky to take them to America."

"Their mother is in America. It should be fine," Jax said, scanning their faces.

"We might need to leave them in Durabia where they'll be afforded more protection. Durabia has become the Switzerland of the Middle East. Vikkas has already sent word to Shiekh Kamran that they need to establish more housing and resources for Ajid refugees from here and from countries who deny asylum for Ajid families and plan to ship them out. There will be quite a few of them. America is having an interesting time with immigrants. The minute they arrive in America, they'll ship Lotus and Fatima right back to Ajid if we don't establish something legally with their mother first."

Alia turned Jax's cell screen to face him when an image of Vikkas and Dro flashed on it. Their signal that they were on their way. "Tell me why Calvin and Daron alone are so important to you when you said there are many others at your call?"

"If anyone can help us to create devices to execute a master plan to get all of us out of here, they will. Vikkas was able to make a connection to get our passports as far as Nadaum, it might take a little more effort to get them near the point where we hit dry land."

"Be careful. Any calls you make from those places will be monitored," Nasir warned, writing an address on a slip of paper.

"We all know how to speak in code. It's how I was able to get Dro and Vikkas here."

"Yes, I heard a little of that first phone call when your cells mysteriously stopped being able to connect with any carrier," Nasir said, sliding the mug off to the side. "The sounds reminded me of the old Navajo Code Talkers I read about as a boy. I found that part of American history fascinating. I always had a desire to visit a reservation because of that. Now I might never get a chance."

Jax snatched up another piece of bread, going for the savory oil this time. "When we get to the States, I'll introduce you to Darryl Benally, an author friend from my time when I needed some insight from a paratrooper. I was the youngest person in the unit, and he took me under his wing. He can tell you all about his grandfather and some of the legends and history of his people. Great guy. Loves cigars and educating young minds just like you do. Though maybe he's not as good of a cook as you are."

Nasir laughed. "Optimistic. I love it. And I would love to meet him, but only when I see Siobhan first and I am warmed by her smile once more." He sighed as a sad little smile made his eyes crinkle at the corners. He had missed his wife something awful. Photos of her were all around the house, a reminder of a separation that was not of their choosing.

Nasir focused on the direction that led to the upper level of the house. The sobbing had finally stopped, and laughter had taken its place. Simi was with friends, and Kamala's whereabouts were unknown—again. No amount of warnings kept her indoors. Alia told them they shouldn't worry since she always came back before dark. No one, except Jax, Dro, and Vikkas, seemed to still have lingering questions about her actions.

"We still don't know who to trust, Nasir," Jax said as Simi sashayed into the room, peered in the pot on the stove, wrinkled her nose and backed away.

"Stew again?" she whined, stepping in from the garden entrance.

Evidently, she had been listening in before making her presence known.

"We have the same thing day after day. When can we have lamb or anything that doesn't seem like we're poor?" She angled to face

Jax. "If you go to the sweet shop, may I come too? I could really go for some of their khir. It's like sin in a bowl."

Nasir crossed the distance and grabbed her shoulder. "Perhaps a night with no supper will remind you to be content with your blessings, no matter how big or small. You are not supposed to be out unescorted. Yet you defy me every time." When she didn't move, Nasir jerked his thumb toward the back stairs and Simi scowled before hurrying up to her bedroom.

"From this point on, no more conversations take place unless those three are outside," Jax warned. "They should be in the garden where we can lay eyes on them whenever we have discussions."

"Go see if Alia needs help calming your cousin," Raja called out to Simi who rushed to comply.

It took everything in Jax not to glance over his shoulder. Part of him hoped to see his wife standing there, but another part of him made a mental note to sit closer to the door from now on because Amal had somehow crept back in.

Once he heard Simi's footsteps moving across the floor above and the patter of another set of feet moving away, Jax leaned closer. "We're going to have to trust someone to get the equipment and supplies we need." He tipped over to position near the stairway and still have a view of everyone else in the room. "Ultimately, we'll have to float to Nadaum, and they'll have to extract us from there."

"The problem is that Nadaum might not be the best choice since they are at odds with Durabia after what Ellena did to their ruling Sheikh."

"But we stand a better chance with them, than here."

"We can only pray," Raja whispered.

CHAPTER 16

*S*ix Days Before the Freedom Gala

"WELL IF IT isn't the Prodigal Son himself," Daron Kincaid teased as he adjusted the screen. "How the hell are you?"

Any other time, the dig would have spawned an argument between Jax and the person crazy enough to call him that name to his face. However, things being what they were, the familiar, gravelly sound of Daron's voice made Jax long for the cold, clinical feel of Daron's laboratory in the heart of Morgan Park, south of downtown Chicago. The place where magic happened. The place he hoped his Castle brothers could create ... a miracle.

Daron owned Crossroads Security, and as King of Morgan Park he was the main one to oversee security for The Castle. Calvin, a brilliant inventor and Knight of South Holland, helped him create gadgets to serve and protect the global organization.

"We need your help," Jax said, knowing full well he would have to face even more ribbing for asking Daron for anything. He swore that he'd never need him again. Especially since Cameron Stone, Daron's partner, had more finesse and had come through on several occasions. Daron was a "blow things up" kind a guy. Cameron was a "solve the problem without anyone knowing what hit them" kind of woman.

Under normal circumstances, none of them, not even Dro, would have any inkling that Jax was in any kind of trouble. He would have handled the situation on his own. The most any of the Kings had known about his comings and goings were found in the injuries he conveniently never explained. They were par for the course in the kind of assignments he took on.

"First, before you even tune your lips to ask, we are not sending any more Kings, Knights, Queens or anyone directly into that place," Daron warned, passing a file to a red-haired woman who was well known for her failed attempts to get Jax in the sack. "It's like the Bermuda Triangle of the Middle East. Kings go in but don't come home."

"That's a little bit of an exaggeration," Jax countered as realization hit full force. With Dro and Vikkas stationed in the hotel most days, and going out only to navigate the passports to the right place and people in Nadaum, Daron's words seemed to be more truth than fiction.

"Lola is losing her mind," Daron said. "She says, 'if you don't have Dro out of that place and home for the wedding, I'm going to fire every last one of you as Kings and put a bullet in every King tush I find.'"

"Will she do that?" Calvin asked, getting up from his computer. His face had that quizzical expression that made Jax think the man was genuinely surprised that a Queen would lay that kind of threat. He had to know how the Queens came into being.

"The Queens can do anything they like," Vikkas said. "Mine put a bullet into her brother when he tried to get over on me and the Kings."

"Well, good thing I'm a Knight, so my ass will stay intact," Calvin said with a chuckle.

"Actually, she also said she was going to *set us* on fire. After the bullet, though." Daron adjusted his signature fedora as a smile played about his lips. "But I thought the way I put it was a little more politically correct."

"There is that," Dro admitted as he held up a hand to silence Jax who was all too ready to jump in with another round of sentiments. "And if you apologize one more time for all of this, I will unleash my fiancée on you directly. She's pretty good with a flame thrower."

Jax scratched the back of his head and winced at the tension that had formed a knot between his shoulders. "Oded made a new dictate that Americans cannot come into the country—not even military. Those who were set to assist us can't get to us in this area. That also means since a demand came for Dro and Vikkas to attend the gala, they'll be detained if they try to leave by normal American channels."

Dro leaned closer to the laptop screen. They were broadcasting on a back channel with equipment that one of Om Ali's connections provided. "We need you to pull some things together on your end."

"Such as?" Daron hedged as one of his assistants came over with a clipboard. He signed a document, and the woman left but not before giving Jax one last lingering look. She'd been another one who was sweet on Jax since he had been placed on the team. Jax wasn't up for the challenge then, and definitely not since he was now a married man.

"For starters, a more secure and consistent channel to have these discussions," Dro replied, frowning at Wendy's slowly retreating figure as she seemed to hesitate while keeping her attention on Jax, who had never taken her up on anything she offered. "We keep having to float from shop to shop picking up new equipment every day."

Daron waited until the door closed behind her and Calvin joined him in front of the monitor. "Not possible given the time-frame we're working with. Use what you have, and switch to King Speak protocol every time. That will work on any channel. It's less likely anyone can figure out what we're saying."

Calvin raised an eyebrow. "You know I'm rusty with that."

Jax folded his arms across his massive chest. "No choice. None of this is for anyone's ears but yours."

For the next few minutes, Jax was able to use complete King Speak Protocol to get his message across about what their best Plan A and Plan B panned out to be.

"Are you serious?" Daron asked, and the tech guru's voice was filled with every bit of what Jax had longed to express the entire ordeal.

"As a heart attack," Jax shot back.

"That's a mighty tall order." Calvin rubbed his short, cropped hair and inhaled.

"It gets better," Vikkas chimed in with a pointed look at Jax. "We also have a Joseph and Mary situation going on here."

Daron and Calvin gave each other a questioning glance before facing the screen once again. "Before Jesus or after?" Calvin asked.

"Everyone will believe it's before," Jax mumbled, giving Vikkas the evil eye.

Daron whistled through his teeth, then his fingers flew across the keyboard. "Let me pull some strategies together on this end and get back to you."

CHAPTER 17

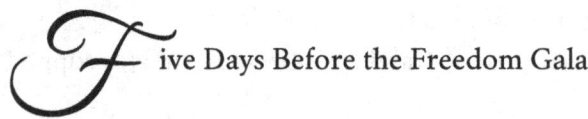 ive Days Before the Freedom Gala

PRECIOUS BUBBLES of life-giving air rushed to the surface as Alia sank to the bottom of the pond in the outer reaches of the garden. Her arms and legs grew heavy with fatigue the moment the crystal-blue water faded to black. Vise-like fingers dug into her arms and yanked her to the surface.

"Alia," Jax called in a rushed whisper.

"Sor-sorry, Jax," she sputtered, struggling to fill her lungs with fresh air while the burning in her eyes nearly rendered her nearly blind. "Let's try again."

Jax pulled a towel close around her and crushed her to his chest. "No, we'll have to find another way."

"There *is* no other way," she countered, her hazel eyes imploring him to understand. She put a little distance between them. "I'm the only one with this problem. I almost drowned in a lake when I visited here as a little girl. Uncle Ibrahim pushed me in and told me to sink or swim. Aunt Raja saved my life." She gave him a half smile. "Sometimes the thing you fear the most is the thing that can deliver you from evil. Life is funny that way. I will master this."

Jax pulled back a little as though searching her face for any hint of distress. Then he led her to a wooden bench where they sat side by side, contemplating all the efforts she had undertaken. At first, they had tried the shallow end of the pool for floating, but that totally paralyzed her. The pond was a better option. But still, she struggled.

Alia buried her face in his shoulder. "We're running out of time, Jax. I'm starting to show and it's hard to hide now. The celebration is only a few days away. It's only a matter of time before they find out."

Though Balitan guards had stopped their rotation of watching the house, Jax escorted Alia back to their room. He placed his large hand over her stomach, and she laid her much smaller hand over his. He kissed her forehead and whispered, "I promise to keep our family safe."

"I know you will."

"The American military gave us as much equipment and assistance as they could give to us without causing a major political incident," he whispered, keeping her close. "Little does Oded know, the rest of the equipment he tried to confiscate from the American military base is waiting for us," Jax said, taking in the lush greenery beyond the pond. "Maybe we can still get the others out by water and find another way for you."

Alia hooked a finger under his chin and made him lock a steady gaze on her. "We already know this is the way. I will keep practicing. I won't condemn our family to a life of servitude or death because of an age-old trauma of mine."

Alia pulled back to see him blinking rapidly and cupped his face in her hands.

"Never thought the word family would ever apply to me again," he said. "Not until I came here. Not until I met you,"

She smiled at that admission, and it swept aside all feelings of defeat. "The Kings are also your family, or they wouldn't be fighting so hard. You have family all around you. Only now it includes my rag tag odd lot of people to add to your circle. You have a whole damn tribe and me and our baby are standing right beside you."

Jax looked at her for the longest time, then pressed his forehead to hers and chuckled.

"What?" she asked, tilting her head.

"How can someone so gentle be so tough?"

Alia sat back and folded her arms. "My strength seems to amuse you more than impress you. Then why is it that I'm struggling so hard with the water? I want to overcome it, I truly do."

An impish smile spread across his face. "Remember when you punched that boy out on the playground?"

Alia clapped a hand over her mouth and giggled. "Father told you about that?"

Jax nodded and bit down on his lip, stifling a laugh of his own. "He was so proud of you that day. You stood up for yourself and sent that little boy running home with his tail tucked between his legs along with a black eye and bloody nose."

She balled up a fist and planted it in her other hand as though sending someone a message that she'd do it again if needed. "I didn't even mind getting grounded by my mother because from that day on, other boys didn't try to look up my skirt."

The indulgent smile Jax wore faded as he continued. "Save your strength, baby. We may need your fists of steel before it's all over."

"I haven't been totally honest with you," she said before filling him in on what she learned from following Kamala that night; as well as about the secret stash hidden behind Nasir's bookshelf which could come in handy if they needed to grease a few more palms along the way. Nadaum would be a whole new set of challenges. Their ruler was now publicly siding with Oded, as well as some other countries who were calling for sanctions against Ajid to be lifted immediately.

"I won't insult you by asking if you're sure."

She nodded.

"Baby, we have to be open with each other. You have to know that I'm going to do what's best for this family."

"But suppose what you think is best is leaving her behind?"

Now he understood why Alia was visibly shaken when he returned that evening after meeting with Dro and Vikkas. All through dinner, she had pushed the food around on her plate but ate very little. She kept eyeing Kamala as though she wanted to say something or slug someone. When she finally had enough of whatever had gotten under her skin, she excused herself from the table and went to their bedroom. He had planned to figure out what was going on with Alia, but first he had to give Nasir the instructions from Dro and Vikkas. Alia was already asleep by the time he slid into bed. Then the next morning a new set of urgent issues demanded their attention.

Kamala and Ibrahim presented too many variables at a time when they needed to be sure about most things.

CHAPTER 18

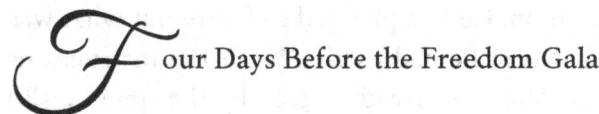our Days Before the Freedom Gala

JAX LOOKED off to the sunset, taking in its array of beautiful colors. No sounds were coming from any of the neighboring houses. "The roads are flooded with people trying to take last minute visits to relatives in other countries. The news is reporting that Oded is not allowing anyone to leave. And he is angered by the Ajidis who are not returning as he demanded. Even those who sided with the regime before Malik are not returning from other countries either —ones who he believed would support what he's doing."

"It's not just us trying to make it out," Vikkas said. "The American military should be evacuated completely the night of the celebration. Everyone else is scrambling to leave before then. Soon, Ajid will be a place no one wants to live."

"From our recent intel, they're repurposing all of the girl's school buildings, making them into holding centers for the women on suicide watch."

Jax glanced in Alia's direction as she shivered from the cool breeze that swept through their home. She'd tried so hard to master the water over the last few days. Unfortunately, each attempt made it clear that she wasn't ready. Probably never would be. If he could put his foot up her uncle's behind, it would only be right. He turned back to finish the conversation with Dro.

"You think something's up with that motive? There has been an uptick in suicides among the Ajidi women. Zaras not so much. They are the ones still fighting."

"I think it's a ploy to get the highly educated women in one place," Jax said, quietly leaning on the wooden fence that walled off a garden that somehow had been maintained and even cleared to plant more vegetables that Nasir loved to tend.

"They'll be plucked from their families and then shuttled off to any of the tribunal men who desire to have them—and not even the ones that have a seat. Just men who have assisted with the takeover and haven't been through vetting by the family on whether they can even afford a wife. This is another way of taking money by marrying into it because the family has to allot a great deal of money for dowry regardless of the marriage's origins."

"Maybe we go out right before the first performer of the concert is set to start since all focus will be on the celebration."

Dro stared over Jax's shoulder at Kamala who was walking out from the front entrance instead of the side leading to the garden. She froze when all eyes landed on her, then she quickly back-tracked into the house.

"Tell me again why the water option is so attractive?" Alia asked.

"Because no one suspects we would go that route," Jax answered her. "Especially since the celebration is going on in the area. Oded's making sure that all of his enemies attend and that they are front and center. It's going to be televised worldwide to make everyone believe that everything is fine in Ajid. They want to prove that all of the information coming from Americans and everyone else is false."

Dro polished off the last remaining bite of garlic naan. "His military is definitely going to be a little lax in some areas, because they'll be putting their efforts on the celebrities, performers, and politicians they've flown in from all over the world. They certainly won't be expecting people to be tipping into the underside of the water."

Vikkas turned his screen to everyone with the news headlines prominently displayed. "Here's something we should consider. Several major celebrities have disregarded the United States level four travel advisory not to come to the area. They are heeding the call of drought-like conditions that exist in some areas since people abandoned their homes, farms and businesses and left very little in the way of providing for their families."

He slid the screen and tapped a spot at the bottom. "Seems like an American producer and his team put the celebration together in three parts—a formal gala with a dinner in the trade center that serves one thousand people—dignitaries and tribunal leaders and their families." He slid to another view. "A concert with several of the top artists in the world performing back-to-back for several hours. Then politicians and leaders supporting Oded would speak to close things out before the wedding to Alia, an outward show of unification of the Ajidis and Zaras."

"Those celebrities can serve as another much-needed distraction," Dro said.

"Or opening," Jax said, with an ear-to-ear grin. "What's the likelihood we can get some Castle members on security detail for them?"

"Love the way you think."

Dro nodded and returned his smile. "We'll get on that right away. That also means that the military on both sides will be stretched thin."

Aunt Raja's face brightened. "And with Oded believing that we are not aware that they plan to take Alia and the rest of the girls that night, he will believe that everything is working in his favor."

"But we still have that one problem," Alia said, and her resigned voice seemed to echo off the stone walkway. "All of you ... just go without me. I don't want any of us to die for my failings."

Those words were like nails down a chalk board.

"I said it before and I'll say it again, I am *not* leaving without you," Jax countered with a gentle grip on her upper arms. "I'm not leaving without all of you."

"Staying might be best for me," Alia said, her tone more resigned than he'd ever heard. "My disappearance, more than any others, will have a severe impact on the rest of my family. You can't know how much I will worry."

"You mean those who will remain when we leave? The ones who broke camp as soon as they figured out that your immediate family was in Oded's crosshairs? They don't deserve your worry, they—"

"We have to go," Dro said pushing back from the table and signaling for Vikkas to join him. "New intel just came in."

CHAPTER 19

*T*hree Days Until the Freedom Gala

"THERE IS a thickness over this place like a scream unuttered," Nasir said, extracting a bottle of sparkling juice from their fridge. "I take it the trip into town did not go as planned?"

"Trip into town" was code for we have news from Dro and Vikkas and need to clear the room so everyone could speak freely.

"Perhaps it will be best to have Alia unconscious. There are medications for that, yes?"

Jax gave his father-in-law a double take.

Nasir flinched as a sorrowful look passed between Jax and Vikkas.

"Dro said the same exact thing. The answer is no," Jax said, and his voice was firm. "Using something to put her out could harm the baby."

"I do not think we have much of a choice." Nasir said as the staccato sound of his knife on the cutting board came to a momentary halt.

Vikkas shook his head. "Maybe there is something to put her under so we can strap on the breathing apparatus and bring her to safety."

Jax held up a hand to stave off any further conversation along those lines. "I won't put either of them at risk like that."

Nasir pushed aside the veggies and slid a garlic clove on the block. "Earlier today, Oded's men stopped by to inspect our home and demanded to have a meal while they waited. They questioned me on Alia's whereabouts even though she was right there under their nose in the pond, and they could visibly lay eyes on her." He peered out of the window into the emptiness. "They wanted to know why all the sudden interest in her desire to learn proper swimming techniques."

Nasir locked gazes with Jax. A weighted silence settled around them before he continued with, "Do not wait for the celebration. You must go tonight. Take all of the children, my sister and leave this place. No matter what it takes."

Jax tensed when a single tear slid down the man's face.

"If you move along the canal's port side," he said, gesturing to the schematics. "Well beneath the water line, you will be able to cross without the border patrols and customs seeing you as you go straight into Nadaum's Free Zone."

Jax glanced at the amber liquid sloshing in the glass and frowned. "I can't put Alia in that kind of danger. And another thing, we get to the other side and then what? Vikkas said that the plans on that side are not fully in place. We'll be caught before we even make it into Nadaum. If the wrong people are waiting on the other side, they'll detain us and hand us back over to the Ajid men who'll be chasing us. We have three days until the gala. We'll figure something out."

The young ones filed in from outside and Nasir held up a hand

and said, "Let us break bread and then we will revisit our problems on a full belly."

* * *

ONCE THEY HAD PARTAKEN of a meal consisting of chicken makhani —a creamy tomato butter sauce, briyani—a rice dice with vegetables, naan—a garlic bread, and a sweet rice dessert that Raja and Nasir had made.

"I need you to stay here," he said to Aunt Raja. "Everyone except Dro, Nasir, Vikkas can clear the room. Kamala and Simi can go too."

Kamala's head whipped around. "Where?"

"To the garden."

"No one wants to go to that stinky old garden," Simi grumbled.

"Why can't we stay and hear what's going on?" Kamala asked flickering a gaze between Alia and Jax, then to Dro and Vikkas. "It's our lives, too."

No one made a move. Aunt Raja hooked her arms under theirs and escorted them to the door before closing it behind them.

They waited until the girls complied before Alia said, "Lotus and Fatima are smaller and won't take up as much space. And they'll listen to you if we get separated." Her voice was little more than a tremulous whisper.

Raja was angled near the door but had a good view of the garden. "Kamala just slipped away again."

"That girl just won't listen," Alia whispered.

"And we actually know why." Jax filled them in on what Alia found out.

"Why didn't you tell us sooner?" Aunt Raja said as her hand flew up to cover her heart.

Jax had to hold on to Alia to keep her from going after her sister. "He will kill her this time."

Nasir stared off into the distance trying to hold in his pain. "He will not harm her. She is still useful to him."

"We've known for a while that Oded probably had eyes and ears beyond your uncle," Jax said. "I'm just so sorry that it turned out to be your sister. The disappearances were a telling point. We could easily track Simi, but Kamala was cagey. What you witnessed that night, which put you at great risk, only confirmed it."

Jax moved into her path and embraced her. "Babe, you're trembling," he said as she struggled in his grasp. Instead of releasing her, Jax crushed her to his chest. "Alia stop."

He braced himself as she gave in and a storm of tears washed over her. "He's going to kill her. She doesn't realize how much danger she's in."

"We'll pick this up in a little while," Jax said to everyone before he half-carried, half-walked her from the room and over to the bed and settled her on the comforter. He pulled it over her legs and snuggled into her. It was a while before she could form her thoughts.

"She never wanted to come here at first, but then she saw how the rich people lived. She became caught up in the glamor and glitz of this place, as if this was her own personal reality show. Even back home she always acted like some modern-day princess." Alia went still then looked up at him. "Did you know it was her before I told you?"

Jax settled back against the pillows. "We've only suspected Amal."

"Which is why we need to speed up the timeline." Alia's restless fingers smoothed the sheet next to Jax. "Have Dro and Vikkas take the younger ones, my father, and my aunt at least."

Jax stilled her hands by bringing them into his while weighing how much of the confidential conversation with Dro and Vikkas he should share. "No. We have to let things play out as they are."

Alia scanned their darkened room, taking in the articles of clothing that hid the pouches that would play a part in securing their freedom. "I don't care what the plan is. We can't go anywhere near that place. Take them so they'll be safe. I can live with whatever happens so long as they are—"

Jax pulled her against his chest. "Wherever I go, you go."

"You know as well as I do, that I can't make this trip, let alone survive it," she protested. "Every single time I hit the water; I became unglued. And right now, it's the only plan we have."

Alia brushed his hand from her shoulder and stood. Before she could take a step, Jax was in front of her. He brushed his fingers across her face. "Your father told me what you'd do if worst came to worst. Do you really think I could go on after something like that?"

She planted her face in his chest. "I won't take that risk, Jax. I am one person and there are many ..."

"Maybe you can't take that risk, but I most certainly will. I'm fighting for my life here and you and our baby are all of it." He angled her face so their gazes met. "Do you trust me?"

Alia tried to push past him, and he planted his feet. She flattened her body against his. The sweet taste of her filled his mouth and his entire being as he returned the kiss with all of the passion he had within. She pulled away moments later, making him groan with pain at the loss of her.

"I trust you, Jax. I love you and I trust you," she whispered while showering his face with soft pecks all the way down to his neck. "Never think anything less."

He sighed and pulled her closer. "Then we stick to our strategy. Everyone leaves the night of the celebration. Dro, Vikkas, Calvin and Daron are working out the rest of the plan as we speak. I can't go into it all right now, just know that when it's over, my mission of getting you to Lola's wedding on time will be complete."

"She's going to be so mad at me."

"Why?"

"I got married before she did. I'm not the maid of honor anymore."

Jax roared with laughter.

CHAPTER 20

*N*ight of the Freedom Gala-Concert-Wedding

J AX , Dro, and Vikkas looked formidable in black tuxes. Raja, Nasir, Lotus, and Fatima wore simple black tunics. Simi and Kamala, however, were dressed in flashy, sparkling tunics that were the brightest of jewel tones—gifts sent by Oded. Alia had tossed hers aside the minute she laid eyes on it. Fatima and Lotus did the same. The rich gold fabric that swathed Kamala and cosmetics that came with it made her look like one of those A-List celebrities she loved. At least Ibrahim hadn't bothered to show his face all that morning. Amal had left the house before they awakened and must have joined Ibrahim at some point.

"Looks more like you're going to someone's funeral," Kamala said flickering a gaze across everyone else. "This is a celebration. Why are you all dressed like this?"

No one bothered to respond. Alia made an attempt, but Aunt Raja put a firm grip on her arm.

They walked out from the house to the brick driveway, aiming to file into Nasir's vehicle and two other cars that they'd "borrowed" from neighbors who were long gone.

A screech of tires proceded three black limos which pulled up to the house and the drivers rushed out with additional guards in tow.

"We will provide escort to the event," said the first one who made it out of the passenger side and on the path.

Nasir's steps slowed to a halt so abruptly Raja nearly bumped into him. "We already have our own transport."

"You will come now."

The guard with an athletic build gestured to the middle limo where a driver waited. "You Americans will travel in this one."

"Or not at all," Jax said, standing between Vikkas and Dro as Vikkas flashed his Durabian passport. "I'll be driving myself."

That brought an immediate reaction from the guards who put a little distance between them and him.

"We will come back for them," another guard said with a dismissive gesture.

"Oded commanded us to bring the Americans as well." The guard with ruddy skin and a thinning hairline, put his gaze on Dro's armful of packages. "What are those?"

"Birthday gifts for Oded."

He stepped forward with hands out. "We will take those."

"They come from America," Jax said, giving the man a smile. "Oded won't be happy if something happened to them."

"You must come with us," the shortest of the group said in a gruff voice.

Only with a signal from Jax did Aunt Raja, Nasir, Lotus, and Fatima slide into the second limo. Kamala and Simi practically ran to the lead limo and scrambled inside leaving the door open for Alia, who remained in place.

Dro leaned into Alia and whispered, "Don't worry. We will

make this work in our favor. You'll know when to handle your part."

"What are you going to do?" she whispered back so only he could hear.

"You'll see," Dro said with a reassuring smile.

She trudged off as he turned to the guards stationed near the limo that had been designated for "those Americans".

"Actually, we have more presents inside the house," Jax said. "It'll be faster if you'd come in to help us carry them out."

Alia glanced out of the rearview mirror and saw several guards following Dro, Jax, and Vikkas into the house.

When the lead limo pulled into the spattering of traffic, Kamala and Simi took fishy-lipped selfies, turning their phones in different directions to catch the perfect angle of dress, hair, and glossy coral-pink lips. They fussed with their already perfectly coiled tresses until finally catching Alia's disapproving gaze, and quickly tucked their phones away. Kamala soon found a pointed interest in a small area at the hem of her tunic.

While Alia stared out of the window, watching as the empty homes that had been part of her childhood faded from view, Kamala said. "Why do you look like you swallowed a whole lemon grove? You might as well make the best of things." She settled back in her seat and clasped Simi's hand in hers, a united front. "Think of all the fun we'll have. Servants and clothes and beautiful rooms."

Tearing her gaze from the passing scenery of luxury homes, Alia asked, "Has it occurred to you that he's only interested in us because of the connections father has in America and because grandfather made us beneficiaries of land and property here in Ajid and in the United States?"

"Then we have something they want. Along with beauty and your brains, it's a triple threat," Kamala teased, her hands raised in mock horror, then her smile disappeared when Alia didn't speak. "Oh, come on Alia, you make us seem like lambs being led to the slaughter."

"The last woman Oded was with, would agree with that sentiment." Alia gave her sister a steely glare which caused Kamala to grimace. "She had to have reconstructive surgery on her nose and eye socket because she had somehow bumped into a wall," Alia said, crooking her fingers into air quotes showing that she didn't believe a word of the explanation that was finally sent to the media. Oded had made the mistake of harming a visiting dignitary's daughter.

Alia glanced over her shoulder and only saw one other limo instead of two. *Where is Jax and the other men?*

Kamala absently straightened her gown as she put a tighter hold on her cell. "Powerful men like Oded have a lot on their plates and—"

"So let me get this straight," Alia snapped, her voice dripping with disdain. "Because a man is having a rough day, it gives him the right to brutalize a woman? Do you even hear yourself?"

"I didn't say that." Kamala pouted, somehow losing an argument that barely began. "Why are you always twisting my words? I just mean that men have a lot to deal with and women should respect that and not get in the way."

The car swept into the marina district as Alia tried to keep her bearings. "Our father never put his hands on our mother, no matter what transpired during the day. How you can rationalize Oded, and men like him, scares me."

"If you'd get off your pedestal and do what's best for our family," Kamala growled, "I wouldn't have had to step in to fix the mess you made."

Alia took in a sharp breath, but realized she needed to choose her words carefully. "And how exactly is that? Do you somehow have access to information we don't? Is that why you were always missing when father told you to stay home where it was safe?" she probed, praying she hadn't somehow tipped her hand.

The fireworks flashed in the sky and all three of the passengers looked up through the sunroof to see the festive display.

"You were making a complete fool of yourself with Jaxon," Kamala said, ignoring the question. "You're an assignment for him, nothing more. You might as well put your attention on your duty to marry Oded and be first wife." Kamala glanced at Simi, who hadn't looked up from her cell since their discussion began. She twirled a strand of hair on her finger while watching the streaming of the performances. "I wasn't a nerd like you, but I could be pretty. Hell, I am prettier than you." She glared at Alia. "If only you would have done what Oded wanted."

"Why? Father gave you anything you wanted. You didn't have to betray us this way. And if you were so on their side, you should have stayed with them."

"They wanted you," Kamala screeched, and the driver's head whipped to her as he frowned. "There was no deal for *me* to become royalty if *you* were not part of it."

At that moment reality hit. This was something more than ego, lust and making a public showing of unity between Zaras and Ajidis. If something happened to Nasir and Siobhan, the holdings —the money, the properties, and businesses in America—all of it would come to Alia first, then her sisters.

Gunshots rang out and the limo came to a screeching halt as the driver jumped out to return fire.

Alia steadied her breathing then aimed the needle at the space between Kamala's bare shoulders and plunged. She gasped, eyes widening with shock before slumping into Alia's lap.

"Please don't do that to me," Simi cried, shrinking back into the seat.

"Don't make me have to," Alia shot back.

* * *

JAX SNATCHED the driver out and tossed him to Vikkas, then ripped open the door, fearing the worst as the limo pulled into the trade warehouse a few miles from the harbor. Oded's giga-yacht was already floating in the water like a sparkling jewel. Alia was huddled in the far corner, cradling Kamala's head in her lap as a single tear shimmered on her face. Simi's eyes were wide with fright and her jaw dropped when he peered inside.

"What happened?" Alia asked.

"Dro and Vikkas took their weapons when we got them in the house," he said. "We have five minutes to get to the meeting point."

"Wait," she said, gripping his arm. "What aren't you telling me?"

"We don't have time for this, Alia."

She moved forward but lifted an eyebrow.

"The ones back at the house are tied up," he said in a patient tone. "The driver and the other guard decided to play hero and now they're in the trunk."

Alia gasped and he added, "Still alive. We won't take anyone out like that unless we absolutely have to." He climbed into the vehicle and sat across from her. "How bad—"

"She's out. Kamala actually thought ... doesn't matter. I know we did the right thing."

Vikkas ran towards them, snatching off his chauffer's cap and also ripped off the driver's blazer that was much too small for his muscular frame. "We need to get going. Someone's bound to find the drivers and guards and come looking when you all don't show up. The last performer is almost done."

Vikkas helped him gather Kamala's sleeping body to carry her. The rest of them piled into one car and were forced to sit on a few laps, but it would only be a short distance.

Passing them the pouch that contained Kamala's identity documents, Alia said, "I'll get her dressed for the water."

"Your aunt is already on site," Jax said. "She can help, we need to work on something else for you."

Alia nodded once, and they moved away from the limo.

"We had Dro drive the cars closer to the trade center so any tracking devices will pick it up and they'll believe that the passengers are at the celebration?"

"Honey, look at me," Jax coaxed from the opposite seat. "How bad was it?"

"I never realized how brainwashed she is." She reached for him, and he carefully guided her from the back of the vehicle towards the trade warehouse. "Now, tell me how you plan to get me across. Will it hurt?"

Jax hauled her to him and stood still for a moment. "No, baby, it won't hurt. You've already been through enough. Come on."

"Wait, where's my father?" Alia asked, looking over her shoulder. "Where's Dro?"

"We have to get to the other end of the pier," Vikkas said, hooking an arm under hers to get her moving.

CHAPTER 21

*L*otus and Fatima sat close to one another on a wooden bench. their eyes filled with anxiousness. At the sight of Alia, they bolted across the room and embraced her tightly, pressing their faces into her side as they babbled on about all that had transpired between leaving home and arriving at the pier.

Aunt Raja finished zipping Kamala into a wet suit and perched next to her to keep her propped up. She clapped her hands twice and the young ones left Alia before hurrying to her side. Simi trudged after them as though in a trance.

"I still don't understand how ..." Her sister's words dried up as a small dark submarine ascended from the dark water and hissed, blowing a plume of water from a mechanism along the top. The familiar logo from an Ajidi oil company on the side

Down the pier at the mouth of the lake, two teen girls rushed towards them, arms outstretched as they reached Aunt Raja.

"What ... what are they doing here?" Alia asked, looking to Vikkas for an explanation.

"We promised Om Ali that his daughters would be safe," Vikkas said.

A few seconds later a hatch opened, and a man with brown skin and short-cropped hair poked his head out, followed by another, both of them unfamiliar. "I hear somebody's looking for a ride?"

Jax grinned as Calvin tipped his way along the side of the vessel and hopped down to shake the hand that Vikkas held out. He gave Jax a casual salute and continued to talk quietly with the man who came out behind him.

Alia laid her head on Jax's shoulder as Aunt Raja walked over. The soft swell of her aunt's stomach protruded through the wetsuit as her salt-and-pepper hair peeked out from the tight black cap. "All right, let's get them on board."

Alia pulled away from Jax. "Board? I don't understand. Where's father? Where's Dro?"

"They'll meet us there," he said, but something in his voice made her alarmed. Then sirens blared in the distance.

"Enough talk," Vikkas said in a sterner voice. "We have to get moving."

"Where is Dro? Where is father?"

"They went back to get Om Ali," Jax confessed as Vikkas glared at him. "He was arrested for treason. They found out that he had been working against them all this time. After the wedding—that will never happen, they're not giving him a trial."

"What does that mean?" Alia asked.

"You know *exactly* what it means," Aunt Raja said, placing a hand over Alia's trembling one. "We have to go, love. Your father would want this."

"Why didn't you go with them," Alia said, flickering a gaze between Jax and Vikkas. "They would've made it back if you all were there."

"Because we both speak Arabic fluently," Jax said in a patient tone. "And we'll need it to navigate our way through Nadaum. Nasir is in good hands. He's with Dro."

"Everyone will be on the mini sub with you," Jax said, gesturing behind her. "I will cross under water with the men to give Om Ali's daughters my space inside. The vessel can only carry a few and this should work as a last-minute adjustment."

Alia backed away from them. "No! No! No! We wait for my father. We wait for Dro. I want to see them," she screamed. "Please, don't leave without my father. Please don't leave without Dro."

Amal was rushing towards them from the opposite direction, dragging a red wagon. Several little boys were also with him and had varied hand carts. A few adults were sprinting behind them. They barely managed to stay ahead of Oded's military who were aiming in their direction.

"You will mind me on this. We will manage." Aunt Raja took Alia's face gently in her hands, but her tone was stern. "We will speak no more of it. The decision is already made. We go forward."

"But—"

Before she could reply, the rhythmic buck of gunfire in the distance made all of them turn and look toward the pier. Military men and vehicles were bearing down on them at breakneck speed.

"Run!"

CHAPTER 22

"Get them on board," Vikkas yelled to Jax. "Everyone else, grab your gear and get moving. Now!"

Amal signaled for something or someone to come forward from the opposite direction. Women, so many of them, took up arms and started picking off the Balitan military. They definitely had better aim and even better timing.

A separate group of men, dressed in all black, moved with tactical speed, and flanked Amal, the rest of the children, and the adults that came with them.

Vikkas, Jax, and Calvin prepared to shoot.

"Hold on," Jax yelled. "They're wearing the King of the Castle crest. They're our people."

Shaz, a tall, loc-wearing man directed the rest of the men to pass him. "Move it! There's a lot more of them. They're on our tail."

Jax whispered the names as their familiar faces came into view. "Shaz, Grant, Reno, Dwayne, Kaleb. "How did you—"

"Go!!!" Vikkas commanded, but his lips were curving upward, relieved to see his fellow Kings.

Amal yelled to the children, "Hurry, get in the water. Swim!" He dragged the wagon to Jax and said, "This should help. Please take them too."

"Who are they?" Raja asked, as Fatima and Lotus slid into the sub.

"They lost their parents, too," Amal said. "They have no one. Please take them."

The wagons were overflowing with gold, diamonds, American cash, Durabian currency and rupees.

Om Ali zigzagged towards the pier. The other men who came with the Kings were laying down cover fire as the Kings took up the task of gathering the wagons and cart and ushering in the women and children. "Where did you get all of this money?"

"I took them from Uncle Ibrahim and Oded," Amal said, trying to keep the pace. "It is what they stole from our family."

Raja hugged him to her breasts. "You were planning this all along?"

Amal nodded. "Forgiveness or permission? The women worked with my mother. They could not get passports or visas. Can you help them, too?"

"Keep moving," Vikkas growled. "We cannot get all of these people into Nadaum using the sub. We have to come up with another plan—and fast."

"If you were able to make it here, where is Dro and Nasir," Alia asked, tears welling up in her eyes.

"They captured them coming out of the palace," Om Ali said. "Dro was out but he went back for Nasir who could not run as fast. He told me to keep going because they would not execute either one of them, but they would make an example of me."

"Sounds about right," Vikkas said, putting a shot into a guard who tried to get closer to the pier.

"These are all the ones we'll need to deal with, right? Dro bought us some time. He is keeping the guards busy."

"Busy how?"

"Dro set fire to the main buildings and the tribunal headquarters," Om Ali said, stroking a hand through his silky salt and pepper hair. "Oded's men left the celebration to protect that area, but they will figure out that it was done purposely soon enough. Then they will come here."

"Did I do good?" Amal said as Kamala awakened and scanned the faces around her, and patted the wet suit on her body.

"You did a wonderful job," Alia said, plastering on a smile though fear was plainly reflected in her eyes. "Your parents would be so proud."

Amal locked gazes with Kamala and gasped. "They have a tracking device in her tunic. Simi too. That is why they are not worried that you are not at the gala."

"Take it off now," Raja commanded.

"I will not," Kamala said inching back, out from her reach.

Simi immediately complied and handed hers to Jax who searched for the device and snatched it out of the hem and hurled it towards the guard.

"Rip it off," Alia warned Kamala.

"No!" Kamala ran backwards until she was out of everyone's reach. Then she turned and broke into a run, straight up the path that would take her back towards the celebration.

Alia started after her, but Jax grabbed her up and Raja kept her from moving forward.

"You cannot fight a battle that she does not want you to win," Raja said.

The Balitan grabbed Kamala up and squirreled her into a vehicle.

"My father. My sister. Dro," Alia cried into his chest.

Simi slid into the tunic that Amal had taken off and passed to her. She shivered in the breeze that swept across them.

"As much as it pains me to say this, she is right," Om Ali said, taking Alia from Aunt Raja's arms and holding her while Raja situated the girls. "My brother knows how to appeal to the youth and to men who want this country to go back to the old ways."

"Temporary visas came through on the American end," Calvin said, holding up his phone. "Daron said the Knights are at the airport base holding ground. The rest of the women who they were able to get out from the American base are being flown out in planes brought in from Durabia, France, and Holland. They're taking off every ten minutes getting the last of the Americans and the Zara refugees out of the area."

"And the Balitan can't shoot those down because both Americans and refugees are on it," Vikkas said.

"Say yes and figure it out," Jax whispered.

"We could not save them all," Om Ali said in a solemn tone. "Some of them were afraid to leave the only home they have ever known."

"We can't have the sub make several trips," Calvin said. "It's a one-way deal. Everyone else has to swim across."

"They'll be killed if they try."

"We do not have a choice," Aunt Raja said.

Some of the women entering the water were bruised, hobbling, but the one thing they also had in common, was a smile as they sensed freedom just within reach.

"The babies can't go over that way," Vikkas said. "They'll need to go into the sub."

"I can make some adjustments for the extra weight, but not much. Two of the adults will have to swim with the rest of the people."

Jax beckoned to Alia. "Close your eyes. I've got you."

Jax stretched out on the shallow parts of the water, then slowly situated Alia on top of him, aiming to float with her to the other side. "No matter what, keep your eyes closed. Okay?"

"They're here," Vikkas said.

"That's all right, so is Plan C."

"Cease fire! Cease fire!" Several of the Balitan commanders

bellowed. And the cry was repeated by several others until the gunshots died down and stopped altogether.

"Oh, this cannot be happening," Aunt Raja whispered.

Despite Jax's warning, Alia opened her eyes. At that moment, the celebrities and performers who were using their phones to film and stream it live to the world, rushed past the Balitan military. They spread out and formed a human shield that allowed the rest of the women and children to safely slide into the water and swim towards Nadaum.

"You said it would take a miracle," Alia whispered, peering through a slit in her vision. "I think we just witnessed one."

CHAPTER 23

Vikkas stopped near the shore and studied the surface of the water. He glanced over his shoulder as Calvin helped the last of the passengers out of the water and onto the opposite shore before joining him.

"We're going to have problems getting all of these people through Nadaum. We only told that man it would be a handful of people," Vikkas said, gripping the edge of a small raft that would carry the babies out of the shallow parts of the water.

"I had to yell for the celebrities to come with us," Jax said. "We couldn't chance things by leaving them there."

Vikkas wiped at the gash on his forehead and focused on the women huddling together. "An explosion pitched the last of the women into the water."

No sooner had he spoken the words, did a soft hiss come to him in the darkness. A lone figure carrying a smaller body on its back rose from the water and walked toward them. The music pulsed around them as Vikkas moved into the water to help Jax out.

"Alia swam the rest of the way herself," Jax said, smiling, then he dropped to his knees and gripped his side.

"Geez, you got hit," Calvin said reaching for Jax.

"Don't worry about me," he said in a hoarse whisper but looked down at the small red circle slowly expanding on his shirt. "Check on Alia."

VIKKAS AND CALVIN gestured at the headlights cutting through the trees on the private road leading to the Nadaum pier.

"We're going to miss the next connections if we don't leave right this minute. We've only gone half the journey. If we miss them, then all of their sacrifices would be for nothing. There are people in Nadaum who are loyal to Oded and his interests."

"Let's go." Vikkas hooked an arm under Jax to help him along.

They reached the border a few yards away on foot, where a young man appeared out of the brush dressed in a black robe.

"I thought there was only supposed to be a few of you," he whispered as he scanned the crowd.

"We need to keep moving to whatever vehicle you have for us," Vikkas insisted as he urged the boy back into the brush and away from the road. "We'll figure out the rest."

An older man with features that resembled the boy's, and several others materialized out of the thicket.

Calvin brought up the rear ushering the nieces in front of him. "We had a last-minute change," he explained to their rescuers.

"This is going to require a lot of work we are not prepared for," the young man piped up and his elder waved a hand to silence him.

"Of course. And we have additional funds," Vikkas said. "You're taking us close to Durabia right?"

"Yes, right near the east border, but we have to make it through the forests and mountains of Nadaum first. Requests just hit the wire for additional money for the capture of Om Ali and the Fadel girls," the young man said, trying to move past his father. The old man struck the ground with his staff, and the younger man backed away, asking, "Should we turn them back?"

"I am a man of my word," Omar said, with a warning glare at his son. "You must forgive my son; he is young and forgets his place. We will take you to your people. We must travel fast. Just be sure that your people remember us when it is our time to flee. Nadaum is certain to follow in Oded's action because they have always wanted their country to do the same."

Vikkas groaned as he tried to keep Jax on his feet. "We have to travel in a way that will put us near some type of sustenance for the women."

Calvin helped to form the women into groups of five, putting the younger ones with guns in the back.

"I feel that once Oded gets a stronghold, then he will come for our territory next," Omar said. "There will be no stopping them. Like an evil tidal wave, he and his regime will wash over us, and they will choke out the root of what once made us honorable men and even more injustice will fall upon our women."

The son said, "Oded always laid claim to this area when Zaras settled here."

"Then why not make those moves to protect your family now?" Vikkas asked.

"I have to come to terms with who I need to leave behind," Omar answered. "Just like you, we will have to leave with nothing but the clothes on our back and the few valuables we have. Starting over in a new country where we have no connections or family is a frightening prospect."

Vikkas held out a hand to Omar. "I promise that you will be taken care of."

"I believe you." Omar clasped Vikkas' hand, shaking it.

"Then you will come with us now," Jax said. "We can detour to your home. Only take what cannot be replaced."

"My wife and children," Omar said in a resigned whisper. "My family. That is all that matters."

Jax looked to Alia, Aunt Raja and the girls and said, "I know exactly what you mean."

OPERATION DIAMOND

"You're dying, Kabrina," Craig warned in a singsong tone while rubbing the stubble of his chestnut brown crew cut. The water level continued to rise and rushed through the ragged remains of the windshield. Even with her strawberry blonde hair a sodden mess and mascara running a marathon down her porcelain skin, his ex-wife still tried her best to look pretty.

"Just tell me what you did with them, and I'll get you outta there," he encouraged as her blubbering grated on his already threadbare nerves. He arched his body in the yoga pose his chiropractor suggested for an old injury as he stood on a rock not too far from the driver's side door. Craig made sure that he wasn't too close to the danger zone. The last thing he needed was to slip and fall into the river or worse, get bested by his ex-wife if she actually freed herself. "Your lungs are going to flood, babe. That freezing water will feel like knives in your windpipe and chest before it's done. We're well aware of how much you hate pain."

"I don't know what or who you're talking about," she insisted in an exasperated tone. "Help me. The water's rising so high," she frantically tried to push the remnants of the airbag out of the way.

Earlier, he had tracked the conniving witch through the airport and ultimately the back roads to the Pocono Mountains Ski Resort, reminding him of the old days when he had pursued her, and she rewarded him with an occasional roll in the hay.

Special Agent Kabrina Adler- Lawson had been a tease right from the start. All he had to do was ply her with a few drinks of the eighty-proof kind and the woman was a fountain of information and orgasms. In the beginning, she was passable for a girlfriend and then tolerable as a wife, even if she had purchased her boobs from some no name surgeon in one of the seedier areas of Mexico.

Overseas deployments and the occasional conjugal visit were enough to make Craig scrap the whole idea of wedded bliss. However, when Kabrina became pregnant, he changed his mind about leaving his daughter to be raised by a woman who wore fake eye lashes and hair extensions. No, he'd stay and be a good father to his daughter, making sure Alexis never knew a second of the fear or pain he had endured as a little boy. No, his 'Lexi Pooh' deserved anything and everything she wanted because she was his princess.

Craig glanced at Kabrina as she struggled against the seatbelt and the steering column pinning her in a dove gray sedan, he had forced off the road. The patch of black ice seemed to appear out of nowhere as they rounded the hairpin turns leading to the resort. When the car plowed through the thicket and slammed into a tree, his heart almost stopped.

She aced her defensive driving skills at the academy, but she was like all the other drivers with their attention buried in their phones. That distracted driving had landed her against a tree with the front part of the vehicle parked in a swollen, icy river. Craig wrinkled his nose in disgust as he took in the last rays of sunlight, making the frigid white-water shimmer like gold.

"Some marriages are dead on arrival," Craig said. "We never should've gone further than a one-night stand, but there I was trying to do right by you. Should've finished you that night."

The pleas of his ex-wife, although distant, seemed more like an annoying mosquito buzzing in his ear than a pledge of undying loyalty.

"We loved each other once," she sobbed as water rushed into her mouth, making her splutter even more. "Please... Craig.... It's... Christmas."

"You always hated the holidays, babe," he countered, rubbing his hands together for warmth that didn't quite reach his icy heart. "Timing is everything, Kabrina. You almost died on me just now." He inched closer. "You were always so selfish. Where. Are. They?"

Craig was overcome with terror as he recalled the sound of Marlon Costa clicking the orange gun safety button on the Glock. All the apologies in the world meant nothing, with a muzzle mashed against the base of his skull. All that remained between a bolt of pain and a lasting darkness were answers he didn't have.

"If... they... weren't... in ...safe..." she gurgled. "Sydney." she struggled with no actual effect on the constraints. "Get... me... out ...here."

Craig let out a hoarse laugh that danced on the razor's edge of hysteria. "You'd sell out your work bestie for me?" He glared at her while absorbing that bit of betrayal. "Of course you would. You sold *me* out. You got people killed because you ran your mouth."

"About... Lexi?" she whined. "Daughter... needs... muh muh me."

He stooped down and lovingly slipped a sodden lock of hair behind her tiny ear. The frigid air and water caused his nose and eyes to burn. "Not anymore. I have a sister. Did I tell you? Haven't seen Daria since..." His words trailed off as he studied the woman in the car and compared her to the raven-haired beauty who would replace her. "My sister will make a better mother than you ever could."

The water streamed around the car, causing it to shift. "Please... Craig," she wheezed. "Won't tuh... tuh... tell anybody."

"Sydney was a better friend than you deserved." he said in an oddly gentle tone. Craig took one last look at the sun sinking beyond the snowy peaks of the mountains that made for a perfect landscape. "And you're right, my love. You won't tell a soul."

He grabbed the back of her head and buried her face in the water.

Download today:
https://books2read.com/Operationdiamond

PROMISE ME A MIRACLE SERIES

OPERATION BUTTERFLY

Jaxon Malone lands the simplest job of his career—travel to the Kingdom of Ajid and escort Alia Fadel back to America to be the maid of honor in their friends' wedding. But no one foresaw a previous regime suddenly surging back to power over the country —or their decision to imprison Alia for standing up to the new rulers. Silenced and alone, Alia loses hope of ever being free again.

Jax springs into action, but every attempt to get Alia out of the country fails. Things go from bad to worse when Ajid's Supreme Leader insists on marrying her in a ruthless power play of a publicly televised ceremony.

Jax needs help—and fast. Several Kings of the Castle rise to the call, traveling behind enemy lines to rescue Alia and her family. But it'll take a miracle to pull off their daring escape plan, which must happen before the new government seals the country off from the rest of the world. Is it too late, even for the Kings, to enact the impossible?

https://books2read.com/operationbutterfly

OPERATION DIAMOND

Someone is trying to kill Dr. Sydney Lomax. The award-winning jeweler and inventor accepts a special assignment from Dro Reyes: transport his custom-made wedding rings across a lake of fire. But neither is aware that the job involves mortal danger. Sydney's enemies are determined to succeed, since her mission across the sands of Durabia threatens their secret munitions dump—where a Doomsday Bomb is silently ticking.

Ethan Wakefield, tasked with finding the government's covert facility that's filled with Sydney's inventions, is assigned to protect yet use her. He must locate her tech, which could save or destroy countless lives, before time runs out. But lines get quickly blurred, and now Ethan and Sydney's newfound love is also at risk of destruction in a deadly game of cat and mouse.

As time winds down, Ethan does everything in his power to bring Sydney home alive—but this time, even his best effort might not be good enough.

https://books2read.com/Operationdiamond

OPERATION IVORY

Michele DaCosta, bridal gown designer extraordinaire receives the commission of her life—except that it's impossibly last-minute. On top of a stressed bride dealing with ghosts from her past, there's also a high-level blizzard attacking all of Chicago, trapping Michele with an over-protective bodyguard.

Rajay Chamani's assignment is to shield the pretty fashion designer from the stalker who ruined a family heirloom and is now determined to use Michele as a messenger to the bride. The situation intensifies when the groom goes missing in action in the Middle East, and Rajay and Michele end up being snowed in. He's blindsided by one more complication: his growing attraction to Michele, simmering hotter even as Mother Nature has the last icy laugh.

Only weeks remain before Chicago's biggest society wedding of the year. Can Rajay and Michele work together to defeat a stalker, defy a blizzard, and finish the world's most elaborate bridal gown to ensure wedding bells win over doomsday knells?

https://books2read.com/Operationivory

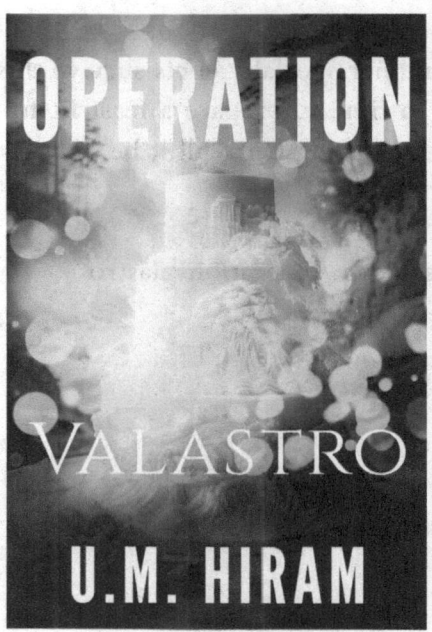

OPERATION VALASTRO

Valentina Romano, a world-famous celebrity chef, is hired to prepare the meal and signature cake for the wedding of Dro Reyes and his fiancée, Lola Samuels. But days before the cele-

bration, she and her four specialty chefs are flat on their backs in an Italian hospital after falling eerily ill.

Dr. Marcus Kyncade, known for his advances in neurotoxins, is the attending physician for the five new patients. His attraction to Valentina is undeniable, but he's shut down by the woman's long-time business associate—and time's relentless scythe.

But to save Valentina's life, he has to beat the blade. He must win a frantic race against the clock to not only find an antidote to a mysterious poison, but also determine exactly who wants Valentina dead.

Will Valentina and her specialty chefs survive this attack from an invisible enemy in time to prepare a feast fit for a King? And if Marcus succeeds in saving her, will it be only to watch her walk out of his life forever?

https://books2read.com/Operationvalastro

OPERATION LOTUS

Noelle Jakob is livid when she's abruptly pulled from a high-profile assignment to locate a vanished VIP bridegroom. The logistics genius for Crossroads Security, tasked with finding the event's missing florist instead, isn't any happier about having to partner with Zane Hargrave. The one man who makes it impossible for her to focus is now her key to solving this mystery and getting back to her original mission.

Easier said than done.

The closer Noelle and Zane's leads get them to their target, the deeper the danger they encounter. With the florist in trouble and the high-profile wedding fast approaching, it's going to take a holiday miracle to align the stars and ensure the event is a "full-blooming" success.

https://books2read.com/Operationlotus

KINGS OF THE CASTLE

The Castle: elite, elusive ... dangerous.

A secret organization which once stood for protection and benevolence, The Castle has now been corrupted by crime, greed, and dirty politics. Every crime syndicate and dirty politician on earth are determined to control the massive fortune guarded by The Kings: a found family forged by fate but called to action by crisis.

When their mentor ends up on the business end of an assassination attempt, nine men are summoned to right old wrongs and track those responsible. The Kings of the Castle, now grown into captains of industry and leaders of men across Chicago, bring their unique skill sets to the daring mission to bring their enemies down—even if they have to rack up a body count to do it.

The job won't be easy, and nobody knows it clearer than the women destined to love each of these men. As powerful forces conspire to twist the Castle's riches for their own good, convictions are challenged and relationships are tested. In the end, will the sacrifices be worth it?

The Kings of the Castle is a series of self-contained stories with characters in a shared world full of high-stakes suspense, fast-paced plots, and breathtaking romance. Each book is written by a national bestselling author and features a different King of the Castle.

https://books2read.com/Kingsofthecastle

Mariano "Reno" DeLuca uses his skills and resources to create safe havens for women in dangerous situations—until a surge in Chatham's criminal activity threatens the safety and anonymity for the residents of The Second Chance at Life Women's Shelter. Though Reno finally admits that the shelter must be relocated, the crisis couldn't be more ill-timed. Just when he's summoned back to The Castle to meet with his brothers in the secret society, a new woman lands on the shelter's doorstep. Immediately drawn to the mysterious beauty, he struggles to refocus on The Castle's newest challenge: an immoral takeover attempt by an enemy who's supposed to be an ally.

Zuri Okusanya, a Tanzanian Princess, has snuck into America with nothing but the clothes on her back and handwritten instructions from her deceased mother. Desperate for refuge from an arranged marriage by her politically motivated father, the princess has survived a near-death experience to land at the door of the

Chatham shelter, unwilling to trust anyone except Mariano DeLuca.

Reno is conflicted. His fugitive princess is as beautiful as she is intelligent, and her plight speaks straight to his soul—not a vulnerability he can afford with so many lives now at stake. Though he strives not to lose his heart to the forbidden goddess, destiny has other plans.

Will Mariano have the fortitude to defeat his adversaries and save the women of the shelter—now including the woman he loves —or will time win and strip him of everything and everyone he holds dear?

https://books2read.com/kingofchatham

Shaz Bostwick prides himself on his moral compass and business ethics–but both are deeply challenged from the moment Camilla Gibson walks into his office, urgently seeking his help.

Camila has no choice but to throw herself on Shaz's mercy. Though she's a renowned blogger for her world adventures and colorful modeling gigs, this is one instance that fame won't solve. Her daughter, Ayanna, needs specialized treatment in Chicago, but time—and the authorities-- aren't on her side. She's elated when the charming but tough lawyer pledges his support.

Shaz, raised as an immigrant, knows the heartache of family separation firsthand. He's moved by Camila's plight, and calls in favors as the clock ticks down. In return, he's presented with a disturbing offer: let baby Ayanna slip through the cracks in exchange for a handsome reward. The call gives him a tip about an illegal adoption ring, but he can only bust the criminals with the help of his brothers from The Castle.

Fed up with politicians and businessmen with too much money and too little scruples, Shaz mobilizes his friends with astounding speed. His tenacity and intelligence move Camila to her core, igniting an attraction she never thought she'd know again—but there's no way she can act on the sparks with the threat deportation still looming for Ayanna and her.

Shaz Bostwick has a fierce reputation for making a way when there is none—but will his legislative superpower be enough to forge a future with his adventurous Camila?
https://books2read.com/KingofEvanston

Doctor Jaidev Maharaj's life takes a dark turn when a coma patient becomes pregnant, propelling him into media infamy. His troubles are tripled when law enforcement and the government join the clamor—and that's before he learns about the attempt on his mentor's life. When he resolves to chase the details, Jai is thrust into a secret brotherhood that belongs to a world he never conceived—and a destiny that suddenly demands more than he's prepared to give.

Temple Devaughn awakens from a year-long coma to discover she has a child—whom she doesn't remember conceiving. The police suspect foul play at the medical center where she was cared for, but to find the truth Temple must trust Jai Maharaj: a stranger who may or may not have her best interests at heart.

As a dark family secret threatens to sabotage Jai and Temple's quest for the truth, they are pulled toward each other in ways they cannot deny—but betrayals, setbacks, and endless mysteries mar every attempt they make to connect. When unseen enemies conspire to silence Temple for good, true values are tested. Will Jai prove to Temple—and himself—that their love is worth fighting for?

ABOUT THE KINGS OF THE CASTLE SERIES:
Each book from 2-9 is a standalone story in the same world, with no cliffhangers.

https://books2read.com/KingofDevon

Two things threaten to destroy most of Daron Kincaid's life: the tracking device he developed to locate human trafficking victims, and an inherited membership in a mysterious outfit called The Castle.

The new developments come with awful timing. After years with Interpol and the FBI, including a sizable sting that brought down notorious criminals, Daron's ready to move on and build a new life with the love of his life, Cameron Stone. But even after years of security expertise, he's not prepared for Marquise Sinclair's treachery. The international crime boss is determined to take Daron's position in the Castle by leveraging Cameron's life against a project worth billions.

Yet even the savvy Sinclair is utterly unaware about Cameron's unique talents: her loveliness conceals highly specialized training to make men weak or put them on the wrong side of the grave. She's not the only one with secrets. When Daron hides key details from Cameron and his inner circle, the deception only complicates an already tumultuous situation.

Can Daron take on Marquise, manage his loyalty to the Castle, and keep deep confidences without permanently losing the woman he loves?

https://books2read.com/Kingofmorganpark

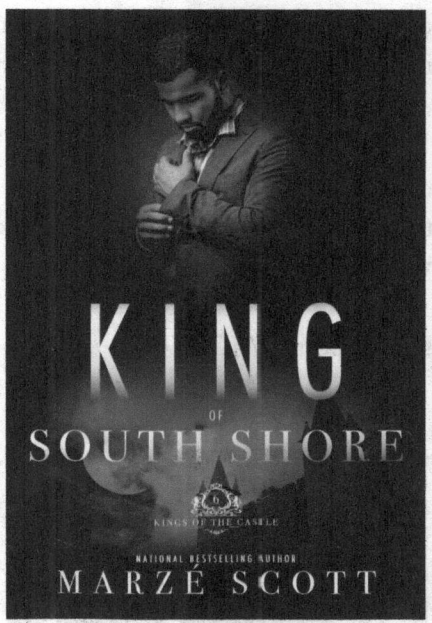

Real estate developer Kaleb Valentine is known for working lifestyle magic, turning failing communities into thriving havens in the Metro Detroit area. He's on track to become one of the city's most renowned success stories—until a suspicious house fire in one of his properties leaves nothing but charred wreckage and five bodies.

Suddenly in the center of an intense criminal investigation, Kaleb is forced to revisit the harsh life he barely escaped as a teen. Life gets even more complicated when he volunteers at the The Second Chance at Life Women's Shelter—and meets a woman who fascinates him like no other.

Skyler Pierson has no time for romance, let alone love—so nobody's more surprised than she when Kaleb Valentine shows up and instantly puts his charm to work on the walls around her heart. But when the dashing entrepreneur asks her for a favor, she's curious and asks questions—too many of them. The danger she'd thought long-gone from her world is back with a vengeance, worsened by mysterious influences from Kaleb's dark past, as well.

Everything is on the line. How far will Kaleb's enemies go to take him—and his new love—down for good?

https://books2read.com/u/4DDl9g

Grant Khambrel, a sexy, successful Texas architect, has worked hard to build a thriving business, only to learn that dirty strings were attached to his seed money—ties it's taken him years to severe.

When the firm wins the prestigious multi-million-dollar

contract to renovate the city's United Center, it should be a reason for celebration, but the past Grant never asked for becomes the inescapable firestorm of his present. Rumors of improper business ethics cast shadows on his company's reputation, intensified when Grant is blackmailed by a powerful local politician.

None of it's the best foot to start out on when meeting the most gorgeous woman he's ever seen.

Autumn Knight, the savvy and beautiful Administrative Director of the United Center, grew up around both sides of Chicago politics. Though her father, a powerful real estate tycoon and alderman, continues to pressure her for under-the-table kickbacks, Autumn is steadfast about her ethics—though that manifesto is harder to maintain when she meets charismatic Grant Khambrel.

The intense man, preselected by her father's committee for the Center's new project, is everything she craves and nothing she can want. Though their chemistry is overwhelming from the start, she doesn't dare trust her heart to a person with such an uncertain past. When more lies and secrets surface, exploring even a casual romance with the gorgeous architect is out of the question.

Will Grant prove to Autumn that he's hero she desires and deserves—or will his tainted success be the ruination of the future they long to believe in?

https://books2read.com/Kingoflincolnpark2

Alejandro "Dro" Reyes has been a "fixer" for as long as he can remember, which makes him perfectly suited to own a crisis management company focused on repairing professional reputations. Business in the Windy City is booming—until a mysterious call following an attempt on his mentor's life forces him to drop everything and accept a position with The Castle. Though his family has been affiliated with the secret organization for decades, his new involvement leads to being blindsided by an enemy he never saw coming.

Lola Samuels, the polished public relations maven of Chicago's elite, sets aside her growing attraction to Dro in the name of seeking assistance for her newest assignment. Longtime bad boy Shawn Mayhew needs some fast shine on his tarnished image: a simple enough job if she and Dro tag-team the essentials, right?

But sometimes, success really is in the details.

Lola is totally unaware of the animosity between the Mayhews and the Reyes —until it's too late. The cut-and-dry job is quickly spun into a sticky web of danger and deceptions—most prominently, Dro's scheme to use their working relationship to gain intel on his enemy.

When Lola discovers she's a pawn in Shawn and Dro's dangerous game, she's conflicted—yet then captured. Alejandro's carefully controlled world is thrown into chaos, and he vows to use every resource in his arsenal, including the skills of the eight men with whom he's just reconnected, to rescue the woman he desperately loves.

https://books2read.com/u/bQe9W7

Dwayne Harper's passion is giving disadvantaged boys the tools to transform themselves into successful men. But when he steps up to take his place among The Kings of the Castle—the men he considers brothers—politics and personalities clash, conspiring against him.

Tiffany Mason is also harboring a dark secret that can shatter Dwayne's ultimate dream, not to mention the depths of his heart. While Dwayne is everything she could want in a handsome, intelligent, and driven man, details from her past have her doubting her worthiness of his marriage proposal. Complicating matters are new accusations against Dwayne, testing his dedication to his cause.

Enter a female acquaintance who's determined to help Dwayne persevere, but her methods become questionable when she uses blackmail to achieve her goals—leveraging Tiffany's scandalous past in her jealousy-driven war chest. Exposed to Dwayne in this insidious manner, Tiffany has no right to recourse, and can only hope Dwayne chooses her as his queen for life.

One woman holds the key to his success; the other will guide him to the cliff of his downfall. It will be the full test of Dwayne Harper's character to discern the difference—and claim his due success as a King of The Castle.
https://books2read.com/King-of-Lawndale

ABOUT THE KINGS OF THE CASTLE SERIES:
Each book from 2-9 is a standalone story in the same world, with no cliffhangers.
https://geni.us/Kingsofthecastleseries

KNIGHTS OF THE CASTLE

No good deed goes unpunished, or that's how Ellena Kiley feels after she rescues a child and the former Crown Prince of Durabia offers to marry her. He is given nine days in order to make her fall in love with him.

Kamran learns of a nefarious plot to undermine his position with the Sheikh and jeopardize his ascent to the throne. He's unsure how Ellena, the fiery American seductress, fits into the plan but she's a secret weapon he's unwilling to relinquish.

Ellena connection to Kamran challenges her ideals, her freedoms, and her heart. Plus, loving him makes her a potential target for his enemies. When Ellena is kidnapped, Kamran is forced to bring in the Kings.

In the race against time to rescue his woman and defeat his enemies, the kingdom of Durabia will never be the same.

Visit https://books2read.com/Kingofdurabia
  to download your copy.

Chaz Maharaj is caught between keeping his public image intact and his heart's desires. The connection with Amanda should have ended with that unconditional "hall pass" which led to one night of unbridled passion. When Amanda walked out of his life, it was supposed to be forever. Neither of them could have anticipated fate's plan.

As Chaz tries to pursue a relationship with her, he's faced with obstacles from his ex-wife and a vicious plot that threatens both their love and Amanda's life. With the help of the Kings of the Castle, Chaz must navigate the treacherous waters of love and deception to protect his newfound love and find a way to be together forever.

Will their love be strong enough to withstand the challenges ahead, or will they be torn apart by forces beyond their control?

https://books2read.com/Knightofbronzeville

When the Kings of the Castle recommend Calvin Atwood, strategic defense inventor, to create a security shield for the kingdom of Durabia, it's the opportunity of a lifetime. The only problem—it's a two-year assignment and he promised his fiancée they would step away from their dangerous lifestyle and start a family.

Security specialist, Mia Jakob, adores Calvin with all her heart, but his last assignment put both of their lives at risk. She understands how important this new role is to the man she loves, but the thought that he may be avoiding commitment does cross her mind.

Calvin was sure he'd made the best decision for his and Mia's future, until enemies of the state target his invention and his woman. Set on a collision course with hidden foes, this Knight will need the help of the Kings to save both his Queen and the Kingdom of Durabia.

https://books2read.com/KnightofSouthHolland

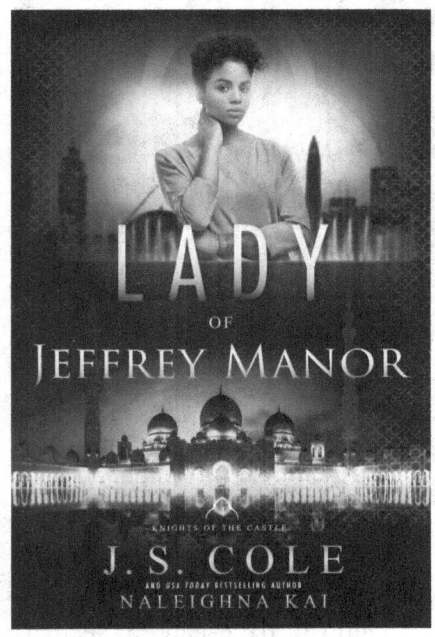

Blair Swanson never expected to find love while on a temporary assignment in the Kingdom of Durabia. But when she meets Hassan, the kingdom's most eligible bachelor, sparks fly between them. Despite his duty to marry for political reasons, Hassan finds himself drawn to the practical and courageous American nurse.

As their feelings for each other deepen, a dark secret threatens to tear them apart. Hassan is torn between his duty to the throne and his love for Blair. With their future hanging in the balance, Blair and Hassan must navigate the complexities of love and duty in a world where nothing is as it seems. Can he find a way to save the woman he loves and fulfill his royal obligations?

Join Blair and Hassan on their journey of love, sacrifice, and discovering what truly matters in Lady of Jeffrey Manor, a heart-warming romance novel that will leave you swooning.

https://books2read.com/Ladyofjefferymanor

Someone is killing women and the villain's next target strikes too close to the Kingdom of Durabia.

Dorian "Ryan" Bostwick is a protector and he's one of the best in the business. When a King of the Castle assigns him to find his former lover, Aziza, he stumbles upon a deadly underworld operating close to the Durabian border.

Aziza Hampton had just rekindled her love affair with Ryan when a night out with friends ends in her kidnapping. Alone and scared, she must find a way to escape her captor and reunite with her lover.

In a race against time, Ryan and the Kings of the Castle follow ominous clues into the underbelly of a system designed to take advantage of the vulnerable. Failure isn't an option and Ryan will rain down hell on earth to save the woman of his heart.

http://books2read.com/KOPI

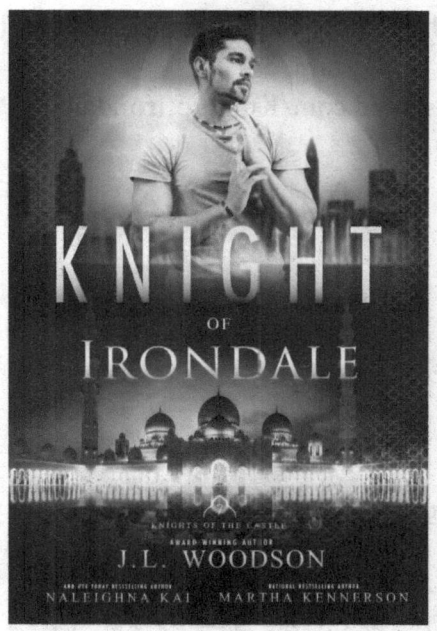

Neesha Carpenter is running from her stalker ex-boyfriend, but now the police have named her the prime suspect in his shooting. With her life in danger and everything spinning out of control, she runs into her high school sweetheart, Christian Vidal, and turns to him for help.

Christian has always been drawn to Neesha's strength, intelligence, and beauty, and he offers her safe haven in the kingdom of Durabia, protecting her from both the danger of her ex and the accusations against her. He enlists the help of the Kings of the Castle to keep her safe, but as their rekindled romance heats up, mounting evidence points to Neesha's guilt. Meanwhile, Neesha's stay in the country puts the royal family at odds with the American government.

As Christian tries to uncover the truth and clear Neesha's name, he must confront the hard question: did the woman he loves pull the trigger, or is she being framed?

https://books2read.com/Knightofirondale

Rahm Fosten is finally free after serving time for a crime he didn't commit. His priority is taking care of the women who supported him during his hellish journey, and pursuing a relationship with Marilyn Spears. But as he tries to settle into his dream life as a Knight of the Castle, old enemies are waiting in the shadows. An unexpected twist threatens to tear Rahm and Marilyn apart just as they are finally together.

Meanwhile, Rahm's Aunt Alyssa travels to Durabia and catches the eye of Ahmad Maharaj, a wealthy surgeon who is on the cutting edge of the medical industry. But attending a private Bliss event puts her in danger and under the watchful eye of a deadly enemy.

As Rahm and Marilyn navigate their romance, they must also protect their loved ones from a vengeful adversary. The Kings of the Castle are on high alert, ready to do whatever it takes to keep Marilyn, Alyssa, and Rahm's family safe.

Join Rahm and Marilyn on their journey of love and danger in Knight of Grand Crossing, and Alyssa and Ahmad in this heart-pounding international suspense novel

https://books2read.com/Knightofgrandcrossing

Single mothers who are eligible for release, have totally disappeared from the Alabama justice system.Women's advocate, Meghan Turner, has uncovered a disturbing pattern and she's desperate for help. Then her worse nightmare becomes a horrific reality when her friend goes missing under the same mysterious circumstances.

Rory Tannous has spent his life helping society's most vulnerable. When he learns of Meghan's dilemma, he takes it personal. Rory has his own tragic past and he'll utilize every connection, even the King of the Castle, to help this intriguing woman find her friend and the other women.

As Rory and Meghan work together, the attraction grows and so does the danger. The stakes are high and they will have to risk their love and lives to defeat a powerful adversary.

https://books2read.com/Knightofbirmingham2

Following an undercover FBI sting operation that didn't go as planned, Agent Mateo Lopez is ready to put the government agency in his rearview mirror.

A confirmed workaholic, his career soared at the cost of his love life which had crashed and burned until mutual friends arranged a date with beautiful, sharp-witted, Rachel Jordan, a rising star at a children's social services agency.

Unlucky in love, Rachel has sworn off romantic relationships, but Mateo finds himself falling for her in more ways than one. When trouble brews in one of Rachel's cases, he does everything in his power to keep her safe—even if it means resorting to extreme measures.

Will the choices they make bring them closer together or cost them their lives?

https://books2read.com/Knight-of-Penn-Quarter

QUEENS OF THE CASTLE

ABOUT THE QUEENS OF THE CASTLE SERIES
Each Queen book is a standalone, without cliffhangers

USA TODAY, **and National Bestselling Authors have created a world where women can—and will have it all—love, family, career, and leave a legacy while overcoming generational challenges.**

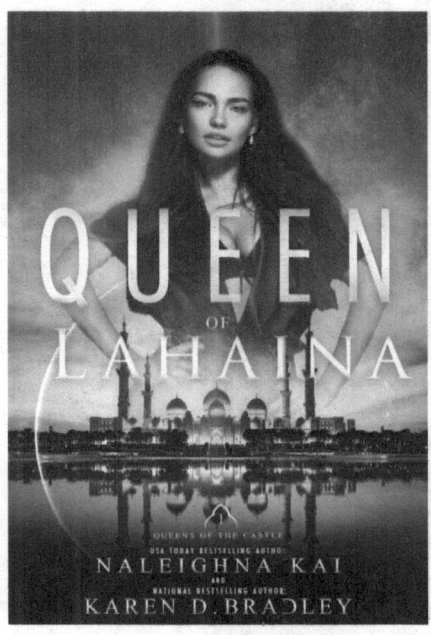

Someone is sabotaging Dr. Lani Jamison's career and their tactics are escalating. Are the attacks attempts to prevent Lani from working with The Castle to implement robotic surgery in the hospital? Or does her association with Jordan Spears have his clients seeking to take her out of the picture?

Jordan lives a complicated life from his family dynamics to his "interesting" career. When Lani tries to distance herself from him, he's forced to temporarily accept it as he staves off the hostile demands of his brother who has racked up debt with the criminals who won't take no for an answer. Will Jordan be able to convince Lani that their relationship deserves a chance despite its origins? And will Lani survive an unknown enemy's endeavor to put her six feet under?

https://books2read.com/QueenofLahaina

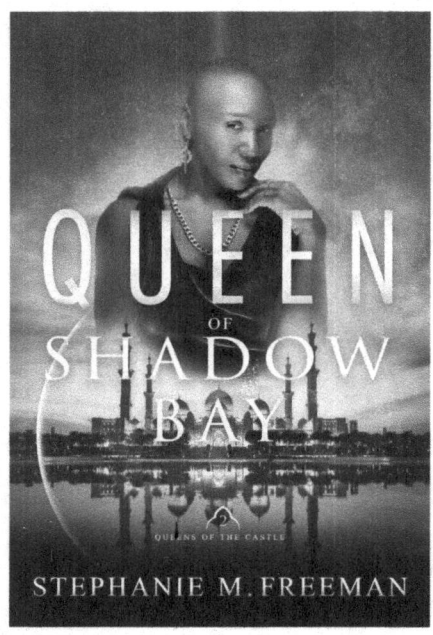

Not all monsters are born, some are made.

Killing Carpathia was the first mistake. Informing her niece made it worse. Durabia meant a fresh start for Raye Bennett. One phone call destroyed all of that. Returning to American soil could send her back to prison for the rest of her life. Attending the funeral of a family member may be deadlier. Heaven and Hell change places in this romantic thriller where the poison is sweeter than the wine.

https://books2read.com/QueenofShadowBay

Solange Porter never believed her husband, Emeril would betray her. But he did. First, he died when he promised they'd be together forever. Then, he left her as the head of a tech company that she didn't want to lead. She wasn't alone; most of the staff felt the same way.

Computer programmer Wale Adisa needs Solange's help. To get it, he will share a secret that Emeril never revealed to her. This secret will not only increase her feelings of betrayal. It may also place a target on her back that could ruin her and the company she's trying to save.

https://books2read.com/Queenofnorthshore

By birth, she is royalty. By choice she is an avenger and equalizer for those who have no voice. When dark forces emerge and threaten not only her queendom but her life, Luiza, Queen of Belize becomes a foot soldier, calling upon the assistance of allies and a few nemeses to help aid in a personal war. It's then that she fulfills the meaning of her name, glorious war hero.

https://books2read.com/Queenofbahia

Samantha DaCosta, reporter extraordinaire, stumbles upon an explosive story in her research of several wealthy, humanitarians connected to The Castle, a place reserved for the mega-rich.

Her uncle, who is a member, has invested in a medical facility that produces and distributes vaccines to third-world countries. The medication has deadly adverse effects, which sets up Ted DaCosta as a target for blackmail.

As Sam uncovers disturbing details, she's conflicted. When her personal safety is threatened, she must either pretend not to know the implications of this nefarious plot, or speak up and bring down a hailstorm of publicity. Danger also stalks her to Jamaica in the form of an assassination attempt.

Kingston "King" Coburn is content to support his woman's endeavors, but when work impacts her well-being, he draws the line. Instead of pulling her back from the edge of a dark abyss, he's drawn into the world of power brokers, who will do anything to increase their wealth.

Only the couple's combined skills and access to a safe haven will keep them alive at the end of their harrowing search for the truth.
https://books2read.com/Queen-of-Kingston

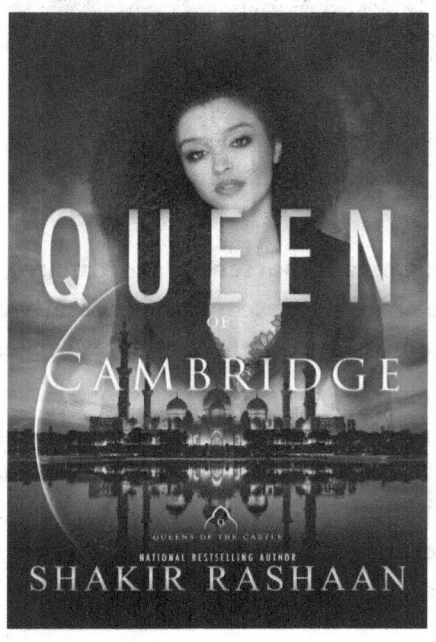

QUEEN OF CAMBRIDGE

Billionaire chocolatier Caressa Sidaná is one of the most recognizable names in the confectionery industry, but she is looking to expand into other ventures.

She is shrewd and no-nonsense, but in her pursuit of business dominance, she has made some mistakes along the way, including the oft-clichéd misstep of mixing business with pleasure.

Her expansion efforts lead to a chance meeting with Ishmael Abdur-Hafiz, an international weapons dealer with the type of connections that could prove beneficial for all parties involved. Their intense attraction and mutual business pursuits draw the attention of a former lover-turned-enemy, intent on ruining everything she has built and permanently removing Ishmael from her life.

Can she find a way to deal with the consequences of her decisions and save her company from potential destruction?

https://books2read.com/Queen-of-Cambridge

Milan Alessia Jackson battled through the scars left in her life from a contentious relationship. Her grandaunt served as her protector and guardian angel until she took her last breath. International lawyer Vikkas Germaine was her childhood friend and true love. Life's circumstances separated them, but his father served as the catalyst to reunite them.

As the couple settle into their new marriage and Durabia, unexpected challenges rise up and threaten to tear their relationship apart. Secrets from her past, an unexpected trip to South Carolina and family members primed to settle scores surface, leading to a whirlwind of upheaval in their lives. Can their love survive these storms or will forces in play destroy everything they're building?

https://books2read.com/QueenofWilmette

Waking up from a coma—without her memory intact—is not something Cassandra anticipated when she says her goodbyes to her best friend, promising to find her daughter, along with the other children who went missing since the arrival of an unknown criminal organization in Curaçao.

https://books2read.com/Queencuracao

Someone is tampering with the water supply in the small Brazilian community, causing many to get sick, including Pilár Silva's beloved grandmother. Pilár leaves Chicago and travels to Salvador, Bahia at the start of Carnival season. She must trust Yoshi Tanaka's expertise as a scientist and his abilities to keep her safe.

Yoshi, an award-winning Hydrologist, is supposed to stay in Rio for a conference, but he honors his brother's request to help a coworker from The Castle who's in the region. In order to keep Pilár safe, he must keep her close.

Danger stalks them like a thief in the night. Will they explore their budding feelings, or will one of them end up in a shallow grave?
https://books2read.com/Queenofbahia

ABOUT NALEIGHNA KAI

Naleighna Kai is the *USA TODAY*, *Essence®*, and national bestselling and award-winning author of several controversial women's fiction, contemporary fiction, Christian fiction, Romance, Suspense, and Science Fiction novels that plumb the depth of unique love triangles and women's issues. She is also a contributor to a New York Times bestseller, one of AALBC's 100 Top Authors, a member of the Chicago Vocational School Hall of Fame (CVS), Mercedes Benz Mentor Award Nominee, and the E. Lynn Harris Author of Distinction.

In addition to successfully cracking the code of landing a deal for herself and others with a major publishing house, she continues to "pay it forward" with the experience of NK Tribe Called Success, the Kings of the Castle Series, the Knights of the Castle Series, and by organizing the annual Cavalcade of Authors which gives readers intimate access to the most accomplished writing talent today. She resides in Chicago where she is working on her next two books.

www.naleighnakai.com

ABOUT MARTHA KENNERSON

Martha Kennerson is the bestselling and award-winning author who's love of reading and writing is a significant part of who she is. She uses both to create the kinds of stories that touch the heart. Martha lives with her family in League City, Texas. She believes her current blessings are only matched by the struggle it took to achieve such happiness. To find out more about Martha and her journey, visit her website at www.marthakennerson.com and you can follow her on Facebook and Twitter.

www.kennersonbooks.com

www.ingramcontent.com/pod-product-compliance
Lightning Source LLC
Chambersburg PA
CBHW011523240626
47154CB00009B/2942

* 9 7 8 1 9 5 2 8 7 1 9 4 8 *